Raising Jesus,
The Early Years

A fictional story about how Jesus,
the son of Mary, came to know and
prepare for his life as The Messiah

*Although fictional, no aspect of this story is incompatible
with accepted versions of the Holy Bible.*

By Bernard F. Barcio, L.H.D.

Cover art by Steve Peters

Barcio, Bernard F., L.H.D.
Raising Jesus, the Early Years
Cover art by Steve Peters

ISBN 978-0-9849159-4-1

Published by Constance Book Project
Evanston, IL, U.S.A.
constancebookproject@gmail.com

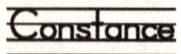

"There is no historical task that so reveals a man's true self as the writing of a life of Jesus."

Albert Schweitzer
The Quest of the Historical Jesus, Chap. 1

Dedication

To my ordained professors at Holy Cross Seminary in La Crosse, Wisconsin, who, as a group, stressed the positive, loving aspects of the character and message of Jesus, and to my own immediate and extended family for providing me with so many wonderful experiences upon which I could draw in creating realistic settings for the fictional aspects of the lives of the Holy Family presented in this work.

Special thanks go also to my son, Phillip, and my brother, Joseph, for their editorial and proofreading expertise.

I am also thankful for the many positive suggestions and comments offered by members of the various adult audiences in Indianapolis to whom I read the manuscript.

Author's Note

I didn't use my original title of this work, **The Apotheosis of Joshua, Called "Jesus" in the New Testament,** because I thought potential readers might find it esoteric and intimidating. This original title, however, does best describe my intention in meditating about, researching and writing the book. I wanted to show how Mary and Joseph raised their son Joshua to understand that he was the Son of God, and how he prepared himself to embrace his role as the Messiah.

I offer the following explanation for those who are familiar with the quotation

"And you shall call his name Jesus"

(Mathew, 1:21)

and may be surprised by the name "Joshua."

When Mathew composed his Gospel in Aramaic, he wrote that an Angel told Joseph in a dream to give the Hebrew name "Joshua" to the child about to be born to his fiancée.

In Hebrew, Joshua means "Yahweh is salvation." But to make the meaning of the Hebrew name more understandable to his Aramaic readers, Mathew also quoted (1:27) verses from the Old Testament (Is., 7:14) which predicted that a child would be born who would be called "Immanuel," a name which speakers of Aramaic would recognize as a simple paraphrase meaning "God is on our side to help."

When the Gospels were translated into Greek, the Greek name for Joshua, "Jesus," was substituted.

The Aramaic word "Messiah," meaning "the anointed one"— Christos, in Greek—was not used as a proper name for Jesus until after his resurrection.

B.F. Barcio, L.H.D., December 3, 2010

How Jesus Learned

(cf. Sec. 472, Catechism of the Catholic Church)

The human soul that the Son of God assumed was endowed with a true, limited, human knowledge. This knowledge "was exercised in the historical conditions of his existence in space and time," which is why he increased in wisdom as he grew up. He had "to inquire for himself" about all those things that in the human condition can be learned only from experience. "This corresponded to the reality of his voluntary emptying of himself, taking 'the form of a slave.' "

Introduction

Having recently researched and published a book of family stories, entitled THAT'S NOT THE WAY I REMEMBER IT, I began to consider just how all the details surrounding the birth of Jesus may have been communicated to the writers of the New Testament Gospels.

Since some of the most interesting family stories pertain to a person's younger years, I was disappointed that the Gospel writers make little or no reference to all the things that Jesus was experiencing between the time he was twelve and when he began his public life at age 30. Those experiences, no doubt, contributed greatly to his effectiveness in filling his adult role as the Messiah.

In this book, therefore, I have attempted to bring those early years to life with hundreds of warm and realistic details and family scenes.

I have also made an effort to postulate fictional but real-life situations that Jesus may have encountered which could have led to the formulation of the Beatitudes proclaimed by him as one of his first public teachings.

Some readers may be aware that there are those who point to Ancient Egyptian, early Islamic, Buddhist and Hindu influences that they feel are part of the teachings of Jesus recorded in the New Testament. Rather than shy away from the suggestion of such influences on the development of the thoughts of Jesus prior to the beginning of his public life, this story embraces the possibilities of such shared enrichment by providing fictional, yet realistic, interplays between Jesus and representatives of those religions.

It is the author's hope that this book will personalize the reader's concept of Jesus and of his Holy Family as well as result in a warm familiarity with the various parables used by Jesus in his teachings when the reader later recalls the fictional settings I have created in which Jesus may have actually encountered the events described in each parable.

Old Testament passages are loosely based on translations found in the King James Version and in the Good News Bible in Today's English Version published by the American Bible Society, New York, 1976.

Table of Contents

Chapter 1

The Handmaiden of the Lord

"Joachim, you must do something. People are beginning to talk, and I don't want our daughter's reputation to be ruined," insisted Anna.

"What would you like me to do? I'm an old man, and he is a young soldier," replied Joachim.

"Joachim, when the angel of God answered my prayer in the garden that we might yet be blessed with a child in our old age, I'm sure he didn't intend for our child to become a disgrace to the whole town of Nazareth."

"You know how soldiers are, Anna. Maybe he'll get bored or get himself transferred. Then he won't bother Mary anymore," suggested Joachim. "And, besides, what disgrace is there if all he does is talk to her when she fetches water from the well?"

"Okay, Joachim, I'll tell you what the disgrace is. Mary begged me not to tell you, but if you must know before you will do something, I'll break my word to her."

"Tell me what, Anna."

"Joachim, our daughter is with child!"

Joachim stiffened. His aged shoulders squared, and his fists clenched.

"SHE'S WHAT?" he shouted.

"Shush, Joachim. We must talk quietly. Not too long ago, Mary confided to me that she, too, had been visited by an angel, just as I had been in the garden fifteen years ago."

"What angel?" insisted Joachim.

"The angel told her his name was Gabriel."

"What else did he tell her?"

"He told her that she would immediately conceive a child, and that she was to name him Jesus."

"Didn't she tell the angel that she was only engaged to Joseph? That there is no way they could be married immediately so she could conceive this child?"

"She told the angel that she did not yet know man."

"What did he have to say to that?" asked Joachim.

"Mary said the angel told her that the Holy Spirit of God would come upon her, and she would be with child immediately."

"Do you believe she's pregnant?" asked Joachim.

"Yes," replied Anna, "our daughter is definitely pregnant. I invited Sarah the Midwife to visit us last week to examine her."

"What did she say?"

"Now Joachim, remember that we must put our trust in God who gave us this child in our old age. You may find what I'm going to tell you hard to believe, but it is the truth."

"What? Tell me, Woman!"

"Sarah the Midwife said that not only is our daughter pregnant, but she is still intact."

"Intact? What does that mean?"

"It means that our daughter is still a virgin. She has not yet been with a man," said Anna.

Joachim said nothing. He just stood there staring at his elderly wife.

"Joachim, we've got to remember that with God all things are possible. Now do you see why it is so important for you to do something about this soldier?"

"Does she know his name?" asked Joachim.

"His name is Panthera," replied Anna. "I quietly tried to learn as much as possible about him before I mentioned this to you."

"So what did you learn, Old Woman?" asked Joachim playfully.

"His full name is Tiberius Iulius Abdes Panthera. They say his mother, Stada, still lives in Phoenicia in the town of Sidon where he was born. He is a mercenary archer with the Roman Legion. He has requested a transfer to another part of the Roman Empire, but people think he may not get his wish for several more years."

"Where does he want to go?" asked Joachim, full of male curiosity for details.

"Someplace called the Rhineland. Have you ever heard of it?"

"No. Hopefully, it's a long ways away. And who knows about the military? He could be transferred when he least expects it."

"Maybe so. But if he's not, what do you think you should do? Once people begin to notice that she's pregnant, you know they are going to say that Panthera is the father. Too many people have seen him talking to Mary almost every day at the well."

"Let me think about this. I'm not as quick-witted as I once was. I will also pray. Then I will talk to Mary."

"To Mary?" asked Anna, fearing that her husband would let Mary know that she had violated her confidence about her pregnancy.

"Well, I'm in no position to bully a Roman archer, so, after I pray and give it some thought, I'll talk to Mary."

"Don't you dare mention what I just told you about her visit by the angel!" insisted Anna.

"I won't. I'm sure God will show me how to protect her reputation and get her away from the soldier all at the same time."

Several days later, as Mary returned home with a bucket of water from the well, her mother asked her if the soldier was still showing up to talk to her.

"Yes, Mother, he was there. I try not to look at his eyes, and I always stay as far as possible away from him, but he insists on talking to me and asking how old I am, and where I live and if I'm engaged to be married yet," said Mary.

"I hope you don't say too much to him," said Anna.

"I usually try to ignore him even though all the other girls at the well giggle and give me sly glances. Today, however, I did answer one of his questions."

"What did you say?"

"I told him that I was engaged to a man named Joseph, and that if he knew what was good for him, he had better quit bothering me."

"What did he say to that?"

"He laughed, of course, and said that he was really scared. Then he asked when Joseph and I were to be married."

"Did you tell him you don't know?"

"Yes, but then he wanted to know why I didn't know, so I told him that Joseph was traveling abroad."

"Then what?"

"Oh, he got all puffed up and announced to everyone that I should just let him know when Joseph gets back because he wants to have a little talk with him."

"Mary," said Anna after Mary had set the water bucket down near the hearth.

"Yes, Mother?"

"I want you to go out into the garden where your father is sharpening knives. Sit with him for a while. He may have something he wants to talk over with you."

So Mary filled a small cup with some fresh water and took it to her father. After she had sat quietly for a while watching him work, she thought she would try opening the conversation.

"Father..."

"Yes, Mary. What is it?"

"Mother said you might have something to discuss with me," suggested Mary timidly.

Joachim finished grinding the edge of the knife as Mary sat fascinated by the tiny sparks that flew from the spinning whetstone.

"Mary, your mother tells me there is a Roman soldier who has been bothering you at the well every day," began Joachim.

"Yes, Father. That's right. His name is Panthera, and he says he is an archer with the Roman Legion."

"Well, your mother and I have decided that we need to protect you from his advances since you are engaged to be married to Joseph."

"What would you like me to do, Father? Someone needs to fetch the water each day, and you and Mother are too old to carry the bucket by yourselves."

"Mary, I have decided that it would be best for you to go away for a little while. I'll ask our neighbor if his daughter can bring us our water each day after she fills a bucket for her own family."

"Where am I to go?" asked Mary.

"Well, I think that that is something you and your mother need to decide. Go back into the house and tell her what I have said. We'll have to see if she can suggest someplace for you to go for a while until Joseph returns from his travels," said Joachim.

When Mary returned to the house, she explained what her father had said.

"Here, Mary," said Anna. "Knead this dough while I prepare some vegetables. Tomorrow you and I will talk."

The next day, Panthera was waiting for Mary as usual. This time, however, he didn't have much to say. He just sat on a bench near the well and stared at Mary, but not at her face. He seemed to be trying to get a good look at her midsection. Self-consciously, Mary bundled her garments around herself as modestly as she could as she filled her bucket, and then, before Panthera had time to say anything, she turned and hurried back home.

"Mother," said Mary excitedly as she walked through the door.

"What is it, Mary? Was the soldier there again today?"

"Yes he was. And he was acting very strangely."

"What did he say?"

"He didn't say anything. He just kept staring at my belly. Do you think he suspects that I am with child?"

"I don't know. But you will not be fetching any more water. I have decided where you can go for a few months as your father suggested."

"Where, Mother?"

"I'm going to send you to visit your cousin Elizabeth. She is quite old, and she lives with her husband, Zacharias, at En Karem. Since Zacharias is a Temple priest, you should be quite safe there for a few months."

"Mother, did you say my cousin Elizabeth?"

"Yes I did. Why?"

"Well, then, there is another secret told to me by my angel that I need to share with you at this time," said Mary.

"What is it, my child?"

"After I told him that I was willing to accept the will of the Lord and bear a child who would be called the Son of God, and that I would name him Jesus, he mentioned my cousin Elizabeth."

"What? Is she ill? What did he tell you?"

"Elizabeth is fine, Mother. In fact, he told me that she was already in her sixth month. He said he was telling me this to show that with God nothing is impossible. That's when I told him that I was the handmaiden of the Lord and that it should be done to me according to his word."

"Why didn't you tell me this before?"

"Mother, I thought I was to keep it a secret. But now I see that it must be God's will for the two of us to spend time together as our babies grow within us."

"I believe you're right, Mary. It must indeed be God's will. Tonight I'll help you prepare for your trip, and early in the morning your father will start you on the road that you are to follow to go to your cousin's house. You must be sure to help Elizabeth since she is much older than you. I know you have both been blessed by God, and that he will keep you both safe. After three months, as your cousin prepares to deliver her child, you should arrange to return home as quickly as possible so you will be here when Joseph returns from his travels."

Since Anna's relatives had originally lived in Bethlehem, she and Joachim had gotten to know the family of a young man named Joseph that also lived in the area. When Mary had been about seven years old, she and her parents had traveled back to Bethlehem to visit her Mom's relatives. It was during that visit that Joachim and the father of Joseph had entered into an agreement, and Mary had become the fiancée of Joseph, to whom she would be wed when she came of age. And Mary was now of age.

"Mother, what will Joseph do when he learns that I am already with child?"

"That is not your worry, Mary. If your baby is truly the Son of God as the angel Gabriel told you, I'm sure that God will provide a solution."

In a little while, Anna went to talk privately with her husband.

"Joachim," she began, "I have decided to have Mary go and stay with my cousin Elizabeth and her husband at En Karem."

"And where is En Karem?" asked Joachim.

"It is a little village just outside the city of Jerusalem."

"Well," said Joachim, "If that is what you have decided."

"Joachim, I need for you to send a message to Elizabeth's husband immediately to inform them of Mary's visit and to let them know her circumstances."

"A message to Jerusalem?" questioned Joachim.

"Yes. Elizabeth's husband is Zacharias, a priest in the great Temple. I believe if you go to the synagogue here in Nazareth and explain that you need to get an urgent message to the house of Zacharias in En Karem, our rabbi will send a Levite. Tell him it is urgent that the message reach Zacharias as quickly as possible."

Joachim set out immediately for the synagogue in Nazareth, and because all was happening in accordance with God's will, a messenger happened to be available.

.

When Mary drew near to Jerusalem and found and entered the house of the priest Zacharias, she immediately greeted her elderly cousin, Elizabeth.

As soon as Elizabeth heard the greeting of Mary, the babe in her own womb leapt, and she was filled with the Holy Spirit. Turning to face Mary, she spoke in a loud and excited voice.

"Blessed are you among woman, my cousin, and blessed is your baby which you carry in your womb!"

Elizabeth warmly embraced Mary and then, holding her shoulders at arms' length, looked at her cousin's young face.

"How is it," she asked, "that the mother of my Lord should visit me? As soon as I heard your greeting, the babe in my own womb leapt for joy."

"How did you know about me?" asked Mary in astonishment.

"A messenger arrived from Nazareth this morning. We know all about your visit by the angel Gabriel. By the way, don't mind my husband Zacharias. The cat has his tongue. He hasn't been able to say a word for six months, ever since I became pregnant with my own child. But you can be sure that we both believe that you are indeed blessed and that everything will happen as was foretold you by the angel of the Lord."

"My soul," said Mary, "magnifies the Lord, and my spirit rejoices in God my Savior. Even though I am his lowly handmaiden, I know that all generations will call me blessed for he that is mighty has done great things to me and holy is his name."

"My," said Elizabeth smiling, "aren't you a little chatterbox! Come. Sit and have a bite to eat and something to drink."

But Mary was overflowing with the Holy Spirit and continued to proclaim the praises of God and predict his greatness in the generations to come before the two women finally settled back into the reality of the chores that would have to be completed for the day.

Mary stayed with Elizabeth and Zacharias for a little less than three months. Before her cousin was ready to have her baby, Mary left to return home. Since she herself was now well into her own pregnancy, she made her ten-day, 100-mile trip back home to Nazareth slowly and carefully.

As she neared her hometown, Mary saw her father sitting in the shade of a tree and looking up the road in her direction, something he had done for many days now having felt that it would soon be time for his daughter to return.

"Fa-ther!" called Mary as she came into hailing distance.

"Mary, my child!" replied her father.

As she drew closer, Joachim noticed his daughter's very obvious condition.

"Take your time, my child. Don't rush. You don't want to hurt your baby."

"Father, did you know all along?" asked Mary.

"Of course I knew, my child," said Joachim as he took her small travel bundle from her. "I'm your father. Fathers know things like that even when they are kept as secrets from them."

"Do you also know about the angel Gabriel," asked Mary.

"Yes. I know that you were visited by an angel just as your mother was when God chose to bless us with you in our old age."

"Well, Father, cousin Elizabeth said that she was sure that my angel must surely have also visited her husband Zacharias as he was praying in the temple. Zacharias lost his power of speech after the visit and never said a word the whole time I was staying at their house. But Elizabeth said that not long after he was struck dumb, she found herself to be with child. When I left, she was praying that God would give Zacharias his speech back after their child was born so she could learn all that the angel must have told him in the temple that day."

"Mary," said Joachim after they had walked along slowly for a while.

"Yes, Father..."

"Mary, I have received word that Joseph will return within two months from his travels and wants your mother and me to be ready for a wedding ceremony when he arrives."

"What will he do when he learns that I am with child?" asked Mary.

"I don't know. But your mother and I trust that God will provide a way for it all to work out. You are a good girl, a handmaiden of the Lord, and I'm sure that you will not be put in any danger for having agreed to let things happen to you according to His word."

The day finally came when Joseph arrived. His trip had been long but successful, and he was looking forward to marrying his young fiancée and beginning a family of his own.

Joseph's initial greetings to both Joachim and Anna were warm and loving. He told them they looked well and complimented them on the fine job they were doing maintaining their home and property.

When, however, Joseph caught sight of Mary standing at the kitchen table, he was dumbfounded. His smile was immediately replaced with a look of bewilderment and betrayal.

"Joseph," ventured Joachim, realizing that Joseph had noticed Mary's condition.

"Joachim," snapped Joseph, "I don't think there is anything that you have to say that I care to listen to."

"Joseph, listen," insisted Joachim. "It is the will of God…"

"The will of God that my fiancée should be carrying another man's child when I take her as my wife? I don't think so, Joachim," said Joseph definitively.

"But Joseph," said Anna meekly, daring to enter into the male conversation, "you don't understand."

"Oh, I understand quite well. I have eyes, don't I? I'm going to leave now. I'll be back after a while to let you know exactly what is going to happen here."

"Pray, Joseph. That's all we ask of you," said Anna.

"Oh, I'll pray alright. But I'm sure you won't like the answer I bring back with me," said Joseph as he left the house.

As it turned out, Joseph did not come back for quite a while.

The good thing was, however, that the soldier Panthera was nowhere to be seen in Nazareth. He had returned to the well for several days after Mary had left, but then just stopped coming. No one was quite sure what had happened to him.

Joachim and Anna kept Mary indoors and allowed her to be seen by none of her friends nor by any of their neighbors. Only they and Joseph knew of her condition.

Late one evening, several weeks later, Joseph returned to the house of his betrothed.

"Joachim," said Joseph when the old man responded to his knock at the door. "Please forgive me and allow me to come in to talk with you and your wife."

"Why of course, Joseph. You are always welcome in our house. Come. Sit. Anna, bring something for Joseph to eat and drink."

Joseph sat for a while in silence, gathering his thoughts, before he began.

"After I left your house on my return from my travels, I pretty much decided to break my engagement with your daughter, quietly. I wasn't going to cause you and your family any disgrace. I was just going to have some documents drawn up, and go away."

"And then what happened?" asked Anna cautiously.

"And then, Anna, as you suggested, I prayed."

"And what answer did you receive to your prayers?" asked Anna hopefully.

"After I prayed, I fell into a deep sleep, and an angel appeared to me as in a dream. He told me that it was God's will that I marry your daughter, and that the child she carried was not the child of another man, but had been conceived by God's Holy Spirit. He told me the child would be a boy and that we were to name him Jesus."

When Joseph said the name "Jesus," Joachim and Anna immediately turned their heads to look at Mary who was listening modestly from another room.

"Did you hear that, Mary?" asked Anna.

"Yes, Mother. That is the same name that the angel Gabriel told me I was to name the baby."

"He must surely then going to be the Son of God as the angel foretold," said Joachim.

"And," continued Joseph, "my angel said the child would save his people from their sins."

"So what now?" asked Joachim.

"Now we get married as we had planned," said Joseph smiling.

"How would you like to handle the ceremony, Joseph?" asked Joachim.

"I've given that quite a bit of thought. If you agree, I think we should let a little more time pass. And then, as though nothing were the matter, we should have a very private ceremony right here in your own home. But as soon as we are married, I believe it would be wise if Mary and I left immediately and traveled to my hometown of Bethlehem. I have not lived near Bethlehem for several years since my parents died, and there will be no scandal since no one will know how long we have been married.

"Joseph," said Anna, "I, too, am descended from the House of David, and I know that Bethlehem is a little more than 100 miles from here. If you wait too long to get married, she will not be able to make the trip safely."

"It will be alright, Anna. I would like to wait at least until August before we get married, and then we shall make our way east across the Jordan River to travel very slowly and carefully south through Perea. After we re-cross the Jordan and head toward Jerusalem, we'll only have a few more miles after that. I will lead an ass on which Mary will ride. We'll stop often and only travel a few miles each day. It will be warm and few travelers will be on the road during the day. She will be safe with me."

"Where will you live?" asked Joachim.

"I will rent temporary lodgings until I can locate a little house in which I can set up a carpenter shop to support us," said Joseph, thinking ahead.

"I am sure that God will protect you," said Anna.

"And you will be in our prayers every day," added Joachim.

Chapter 2

The Holy Family in Bethlehem

Although it was warm outside, the cave in which they had obtained permission to stay was cool. Mary was remarkably calm for a young mother-to-be, and when the time came, she spoke quietly to Joseph.

"Joseph, I think I'm ready."

"I will tell the wife of the Inn Keeper," said Joseph. "She said she had friends who would hurry to help when your time came."

"Are you in pain?" he asked when he returned.

"No," Mary replied. "Nothing really hurts. I just know that I'm ready to have my baby."

In no time at all, two ladies came bustling into the cave and shooed Joseph out.

They quickly fixed a soft place for Mary on some straw and spread a clean mantle over it. As Mary lay down and tried to get comfortable, she smiled.

One of the ladies was ready with cool, wet cloths to lay on Mary's forehead, and offered her hand for Mary to squeeze while the other woman prepared to assist with the delivery.

"Squeeze my hand as hard as you like," said the first woman. "That will help with the pain."

"Thank you," said Mary, continuing to smile peacefully. "But I feel just fine."

And as unbelievable as it may seem, Mary's delivery of her child was as peaceful and painless as God had intended before Adam and Eve fell from grace in the Garden of Eden.

Stunned by the ease of the delivery they had just witnessed, the two women could not help but wonder who this special young girl was and what wonders were predicted by the very unusual delivery they had just helped her complete.

A gentle smack on the behind, and the newborn baby gave its first cry—a joy and relief to all three women and to Joseph who was listening outside near the entrance to the cave. One of the ladies quickly tied and cut the little cord. The other gently cleaned the infant and wrapped it in a warm blanket before placing it in the welcoming arms of its mother to receive his first taste of human milk.

In no time at all, the ladies had changed Mary's clothing and had placed a fresh cloak down on which she could lie while nursing her child.

When Joseph was called in to see the child, he immediately began looking around the cave for something in which it would be able to sleep safely. He brought over a small manger with short legs and placed some clean straw in it. Over the straw he placed a small blanket and then moved the manger near where mother and child lay resting.

After the ladies finished all they needed to do, Joseph thanked them and then double checked to be sure that the ox that was in the cave was secured in its stall and that the ass they had used on the journey was also tied up and had a supply of fodder and water.

Once Mary and the baby were resting quietly, Joseph stepped back outside and found a comfortable spot to collect his thoughts and say a prayer of thanksgiving to God for helping them have a safe trip and for helping Mary safely deliver the child to be named Jesus.

To Joseph, it seemed as though he had just nodded off (although he had, in fact, been asleep for more than a couple hours) when he heard voices approaching the cave. Instinctively, he leapt up to protect the entrance.

"Greetings," said several voices in unison.

"Good evening," said Joseph cautiously eyeing a small group of shepherds.

"Do you know where there is a baby that was just born this evening?" asked one of the younger shepherds.

"Why do you ask?" responded Joseph still not sure what the group wanted.

"Friend," replied another of the shepherds, an older man. "We mean no harm. We were all watching our sheep on those hills in the distance when they suddenly lit up with a bright light, and we all saw an angel of the Lord standing in our midst."

"When he saw that we were all frightened," continued the younger shepherd who had spoken first, "he told us not to be afraid. That he had come to bring us some great news that everyone would be happy to hear."

"And what news was that?" asked Joseph, becoming more comfortable with the group.

"He said that a baby had just been born in the city of David," said a third shepherd who moved forward from the back of the group.

"He said the baby would be anointed by the Lord and would be a Savior," said yet another of the shepherds.

"And then the whole sky seemed to fill with angels who were praising God and singing, 'Glory to God in the highest and, on earth, peace and good well to men.' I tell you, Sir, it was something to see," said the third shepherd who had spoken.

"So, Friend," said the older shepherd, "has a baby by chance been born near here that you know of?"

"Yes," said Joseph. "My wife has just given birth to a baby boy."

"And would he, by chance, be wrapped in a baby blanket and lying in a manger?" continued the older shepherd.

"Yes, I believe he is," said Joseph. "Would you like to see?"

"Indeed we would," said several of the shepherds in unison.

"Wait here," said Joseph, "while I make sure my wife is ready to receive visitors."

When they were invited into the cave, the shepherds quietly and respectfully shuffled forward to take turns looking at the baby and his young mother. The more adventurous extended a friendly finger and brushed the child's cheek or patted its little chest to try and get a reaction from the baby.

After they had all had a chance to see the child, the older shepherd spoke for the group.

"May God bless you both and your child! We know that he is destined for greatness, and we thank you for allowing us to see what was foretold to us by the angel on the hill."

At that point, the shepherds began to file slowly from the cave. As soon as they were a respectable distance away from the entrance, they could be heard glorifying God and discussing what had been told to them on the hill and what they had seen in the cave.

Over the next few days, as the shepherds spread the word about the child in the cave, more and more people began to visit.

Mary would awake each morning to the sound of turtledoves cooing in the trees outside their cave. She would wake baby Jesus with a kiss and ask him if he could hear them.

"They're my favorite little birds. They're saying, 'We love you, Jesus! We love you, Jesus!' Do you hear them?

Baby Jesus would smile and open his little arms to hug his mommy and make her day special.

As the day's visitors began to arrive, they brought baskets of food for the young couple and asked if they could please see the child. Joseph and Mary welcomed all their visitors and, when awake and not being fed, the baby Jesus was pleasant and smiled easily at everyone who leaned over his little manger to talk to him or to let him grasp one of their fingers with his small hand.

After eight days, Joseph and Mary took the child to the local synagogue, where he was circumcised by the rabbi and named Jesus.

As soon as things were a little less hectic in Bethlehem, Joseph was able to locate a nice little place near the outskirts of town where they could set up housekeeping and he could begin to accept carpenter work to support his family.

Together they kept a careful count as the days passed because they knew that, according with the laws of Moses, Jesus would need to be presented in the Temple at Jerusalem on the 40th day after his birth.

When the big day finally arrived, Joseph prepared the ass for the trip while Mary dressed herself in her best garments and bundled up her child.

"When we get to the Temple, Joseph, shall we offer two turtledoves or two pigeons for the ceremony?" asked Mary.

"Which do you prefer?"

"If they are available, I would prefer two turtledoves," said Mary. "They are such peaceful little birds."

"We'll have to see if they are available," said Joseph. "I guess if they're not, we'll just have to go with two pigeons."

There was not much traffic on the road into Jerusalem, and the morning was cool so within two hours of leaving their cave in Bethlehem, Joseph was helping Mary down and securing the ass to one of the many hitching posts near the Temple precinct.

Joseph saw a vendor who was selling turtledoves and quickly completed his purchase. He then led his little family into the Temple.

No sooner had they entered the Temple than an elderly gentleman approached Mary.

"The Lord be praised," said the elderly gentleman as soon as he saw the baby in her arms.

"The Lord be praised," said Mary echoing his prayer.

"Madam," said the elderly man, "I am Simeon. For many years I have been waiting for the consolation of Israel. I came to the temple this morning because the Holy Spirit, which has assured me that I would not die before I had seen the Lord's anointed one, told me to do so. The Holy Spirit now tells me that your child is the one I have been waiting to see."

"Simeon," said Joseph, " my name is Joseph. This is my wife Mary and the infant we have named Jesus. We thank you for your kind words, and we trust that the Holy Spirit is indeed with you."

"May I please hold him?" asked Simeon.
When Mary gently placed the baby Jesus in the arms of Simeon, the face of the elderly gentleman beamed.

"Blessed be you, oh Lord," began Simeon. "I, your servant, am now ready to die in peace for my eyes have seen the salvation you have prepared before all people."

Joseph and Mary stood in amazement as they listened and watched Simeon holding the child in his arms.

"A light," continued Simeon, "for the Gentiles and the glory of your people Israel."

Then, looking directly at her, Simeon addressed the child's mother.

"Your child will cause the fall and rising of many in Israel. He shall have enemies, and your own heart will be pierced with sorrow. Through him the thoughts of many hearts will be revealed."

As Simeon was handing the infant Jesus back to Mary, a very old prophetess named Anna came up and looked at the child. As a widow, Anna had served God fasting and praying night and day in the temple for 84 years. After taking a long look at the baby Jesus, she spoke.

"What is the child's name?" she asked.

"His name is Jesus," said Joseph.

Anna immediately began to give thanks to the Lord and, as she walked away, she stopped all those who were looking for redemption in Jerusalem and told them about the child named Jesus that she had just seen.

When Joseph and Mary performed all things the law required, they left the Temple and began the five-mile journey back to their little house and workshop in Bethlehem.

Like all parents, Mary and Joseph were thrilled the first time they heard Jesus say "Amma" or "Abba." And, once he was able to stand up by himself, they spent many evenings encouraging him to walk, very unsteadily at first, from one to the other as they made a game of catching him as soon as got close enough or helping him back up if he took a flop.

About two years later, Joseph was surprised to see, once again, the older shepherd who had visited them in the cave on the night on which Jesus had been born.

"Greetings," said the friendly voice.

"Welcome," said Joseph recognizing the shepherd immediately.

"Are mother and child well?" asked the shepherd.

"Yes, God be blessed," said Joseph. "They are both well."

"I had a little trouble finding you," smiled the shepherd. "Are your wife and child here with you in this little house?"

"Yes," said Joseph. "Why do you ask?"

"Friend," continued the shepherd, "I have been hired by three very wealthy travelers from the east to bring them here to see the child."

"How do they know about him?" asked Joseph.

"They are Magi, and they say that they were led to Jerusalem by their observation of the stars that told them that a new King of the Jews was to be born."

"How did they know to come here to Bethlehem," asked Joseph.

"As is proper for wealthy foreign visitors, they went first to pay their respects to King Herod and to ask him if he knew of the birth of such a child. The king quickly put his staff to work doing some research, and they told the visitors that the most likely place to look would be in the city of Bethlehem."

"That is correct," said a strong, cultured and authoritative voice behind the shepherd.

Joseph looked up to see what was obviously a very wealthy older man accompanied by several servants. Although Joseph was well traveled himself, he was temporarily dumbfounded by the splendor of his visitor.

"We were told," continued the wealthy visitor, "that according to a prophet, this House of Bread, known as Bethlehem, was not the least among the cities in Juda because from it would come a Governor to rule the people of Israel. When we came near your city, we asked shepherds we met along the road if any knew of the birth of such a child. It was then that this gentleman agreed to be our guide."

"Our child is named Jesus," began Joseph, finally finding his voice, "and my wife and I would be honored to have you see him." He then pointed the way into the house.

By this time, all three of the Magi were gathered before the entrance with their servants and caravan animals. The Magi gave instructions to their servants to bring them the gifts they had brought for the child and then told them all to wait outside while they went in.

Mary was amazed by the splendor of their visitors, but realizing the importance of her child, she accepted their visit as something that was his due, and she gladly presented her little baby boy to the Magi, and accepted their generous gifts.

The next day, the older shepherd paid Joseph an unexpected very early morning visit.

"Good morning, friend," said the shepherd in a low voice as he approached Joseph who was gathering kindling near his house.

"Good morning," said Joseph. "You're up early. Is everything all right? Have the Magi you were guiding already started on their trip back as they planned?"

"Well, friend, that's what I came to warn you about," said the shepherd.

"What has happened?"

"Nothing yet. And maybe nothing will come of it, but I thought I should let you know anyway. It may concern your safety."

"What is it? Did something happen to our visitors?"

"No, I believe they are safely on their way. But you see, Friend, they were supposed to return to Jerusalem to let King Herod know where the child was that the prophets predicted would be born in Bethlehem."

"And?" asked Joseph.

"Well, early last night, they say they were warned in a dream not to return to King Herod but to hurry back to their country by an alternate route. They sent a servant to me in the middle of the night. After they explained their change of plans, they asked me to guide them to a road that would allow them to return home without passing through Jerusalem."

"And why are you afraid for our safety?" asked Joseph. "The Magi fear that when King Herod realizes that they have left the country without sharing the whereabouts of the child with him, he may send soldiers to look for you and perhaps threaten the safety of the mother and the child."

"Thank you, my friend," said Joseph. "I'll think about your warning and decide what we shall do."

As the day went on, Mary noticed that Joseph seemed to have something on his mind, but, when asked, he insisted that everything was fine and that there was nothing to worry about.

That night, however, as soon as Joseph fell into his first deep sleep, an angel of the Lord appeared to him.

"Joseph," said the angel, "wake up and flee into Egypt with the child and his mother because King Herod intends to send soldiers to find your child and destroy him. Stay in Egypt until I let you know it is safe to return."

Joseph awoke with a start. He took a minute or two to orient himself and then quickly woke Mary and explained what they needed to do. Before an hour had passed, Joseph had packed his tools and loaded their few belongings and whatever food they had into packs to be slung over the ass and then helped Mary and her child to get comfortable on its back. Then, moving as quietly as they could, they started out in the dark along the road they would need to travel for six days to get across the border into Egypt.

It would be two years before Herod would die and Joseph would receive word that it would be safe for them to return, not to Bethlehem, but to Mary's hometown of Nazareth. By then, Joseph felt that enough time had passed that he would be able to reopen his carpenter's shop in Nazareth and live with his family without raising any eyebrows or causing any talk about the circumstances of their marriage.

Chapter 3

Joseph's Workshop in Nazareth

Joseph had begun the day in his workshop accepting two new orders for chairs, and one order for a small table. He had also accepted a bench to be repaired, one leg of which was broken. Once the orders were in, he had picked one of the projects on which to begin working with a six-year-old boy at his side.

The boy was unusually bright, very talented and clever with his small hands. He was eager to learn all he could about woodworking. In fact, he wanted to learn how to do everything that he saw Joseph doing. Joseph usually only had to show him how to do a new task once or twice before the boy could be relied on to handle it on his own.

After Joseph split several large, cured boards to begin work on the small table, he set the boy to work planing the boards flat and then rubbing them down with sand to produce a smooth finish. As the boards were handed back to him, Joseph began measuring and marking them for final cuts before any needed holes would be bored into them.

They had rested briefly at midday for a snack and a little something to drink,

"Listen, Father!" said the boy. "Do you hear the turtledoves? When I was little, Mom always used to tell me that they were saying, 'We love you! We love you!' Can you hear it?"

"Yes," said Joseph smiling. "That is exactly what it sounds like they are saying. They're your Mother's favorite birds, you know."

"Yes," said the boy. "She has told me many times how you both offered two turtledoves in the temple the first time you took me there after I was born."

"They're very timid little birds and especially loved by Our Father in Heaven."

"I love them too," said the boy. "I don't think I could ever harm one."

Soon, however, the two returned to their tools and went right back to work.

By the time they left their workshop for their evening meal and prayers, the small table stood proudly on the work bench, needing only to be rubbed with oil when they returned the next day. That would be the boy's job.

The boy's name was Jesus.

When the two entered the dining area of their small home, Mary, now a very striking 20-year old young lady, had the evening food prepared.

"Be sure to scrub under those finger nails," instructed Mary as Jesus waited his turn at the washbasin.

Although she knew he was still a little boy who needed almost constant attention and instruction and occasional reprimands when he was found doing things that she and Joseph did not think he was ready to handle yet, she remained in silent awe of him. Always in the back of her mind were the prophecies that both she and Joseph had received prior to his miraculous conception and birth. This curly haired little boy who hummed a little tune as he now stood carefully scrubbing his hands in the washbasin would be the Savior of the World.

After dinner and prayers were complete, Mary brought out her sewing basket and took her seat near the hearth as Joseph added a few more sticks of scrap wood to the fire and brought out a Hebrew text which he was teaching his precocious stepson to read.

Although most men in the little town of Nazareth could not read, it was a skill that Joseph had been privileged to acquire earlier in his life. It was a skill he was now proud to be able to help his stepson master. Although Joseph was too poor to own a scriptural scroll, he had managed to borrow a small one from the simple house that served as a synagogue in Nazareth.

"Jesus," said Joseph, "why don't you light the oil lamp since it's rather dark this evening."

Jesus was always glad to be given a special chore and quickly took an oil lamp from the shelf. He made sure the wick was adjusted properly and that there was oil in the bowl. He then lit a small stick from the fire and used it to ignite the wick. When he finished, he placed the oil lamp down on the hearth.

"Son," said Mary. "Don't put the oil lamp down there."

"Where should I put it?" asked Jesus.

"Put it here on this lamp stand next to the table," said Joseph. "If you're going to light a lamp, you shouldn't hide its light. You need to put it where it can give light to everyone in the house."

Jesus carefully moved the lamp to the stand.

"Now, isn't that better?" asked Mary. "Now I can see my sewing, and you and Joseph can see to read."

"Yes, Mother," said Jesus.

Joseph then placed a small scroll on the table and handed Jesus a wooden pointer to use as he followed the words so he wouldn't dirty the scroll by touching it with his fingers.

"Dad," said Jesus after he had read almost a half a page, carefully following the words from right to left, "tell me again about all the shepherds that came to see me when I was born."

"You never tire of hearing that story, do you?" said Joseph.

"I think it's wonderful how they heard the angels' voices from the sky and came to our little cave in Bethlehem."

"Well, I tell you what. I'll tell you about the shepherds, if your mom will tell you about the three Magi who visited you when you were two years old."

"Will you, Mom?"

"You start, Joseph," said Mary, "and if this young man is still awake when you finish, I'll tell about the beautiful gifts that we got from the Magi."

And so, Joseph would begin, starting with the reason he usually gave for their trip from Nazareth to Bethlehem (that he had to report to his hometown to take part in a census or pay taxes or some other politically inspired reason). Then he would tell how impossible it was to find regular lodging, and how they finally agreed to rent space in a cave that was also used to stable animals, complete with pens and wooden feeding troughs.

"Wasn't it smelly in there?" asked Jesus.

"It was dry and cool, and since you were about ready to be born, we really didn't have much choice. And besides, since it was August and still very warm, the only animals actually in the cave that night were an ox and the ass on which your mother had ridden. There was also a small sheepfold at one end of the cave, but the sheep had been taken out into the countryside to graze in the cool of the evening."

"And you and Mom were comfortable in the cave?" asked Jesus.

"Quite comfortable! And you were such a good baby that you didn't cause your mom any pain when you were born."

"Is that true, Mom?" asked Jesus.

"Yes, it is," said Mary. "You were very good!"

"And since the shepherds had their sheep out in the countryside, that was why an angel had to visit them to tell them where to look for us," observed Jesus. "Mom, did you really lay me in a manger after I was born?"

"Well, I did, but your father had placed a small blanket under you, and you were well wrapped so you wouldn't have to lie directly on the prickly straw. But who knows how many little bugs were hiding down in the bottom of that manger!"

"I like bugs. I think they are the neatest little things. It's too bad they bite us sometimes," said Jesus.

For a while the three of them sat quietly as Mary worked on her sewing, and Joseph and Jesus watched the fire.

"Dad," said Jesus after a while, "If you belong to the House of David as you have told me and I was born in Bethlehem, why did we move to Egypt?"

Joseph looked up at Mary, and they both stared at each other for a while. The question they had long dreaded had finally been asked. It would eventually have to be answered. But not on this night.

"When you get a little older, Son, we'll explain everything more carefully to you," said Mary.

"I'm already six years old, and I'll be seven next August," countered Jesus.

"Well, maybe when you turn seven, you'll be ready to understand," said Mary. "Now don't you think it's time for bed? You and Joseph have a long, hard day ahead of you tomorrow."

"And I'll rub the new table down with oil the first thing tomorrow morning. I'll bet it'll look great!" said Jesus.

"Don't forget to say your prayers, Son," said Mary.

"I won't. 'Night, Mom. 'Night, Dad."

"Sleep tight," said Mary and Joseph in unison.

Jesus spent the rest of that year working along side Joseph while also becoming a very good student of the scriptural scrolls. Not only did he read and discuss passages with Joseph each evening, using small scrolls that Joseph borrowed, but also on those days when he was sent to read and study with a few other boys who were also learning to read under the guidance of the teacher in the small house that served as a synagogue.

Jesus seemed naturally to take a special interest in those scriptures that foretold the coming of a Messiah. He also loved to start discussions about how all the laws of the scriptures might be simplified into one or two statements that would be easy for everyone to remember.

One evening as Jesus sat talking with Joseph after dinner, he mentioned that he had come across a very interesting passage in the scroll of Micah that he and other children were reading that day with their teacher.

"And what passage was that?" asked Joseph.

"It said," began Jesus, reciting the passage by heart, " 'But you, Bethlehem in the district of Ephratah, although you are one of the smallest towns in Juda, yet from you I shall bring a ruler for my people Israel, whose family can be traced back to the days of old." (*Micah 5.2*)

"And why do you find the passage so interesting?" asked Joseph.

"Well, because you and Mom said that I was born in Bethlehem," replied Jesus.

For a while Joseph, Mary and Jesus sat is silence. Mary stopped the handwork on which she was working to look at her son. Joseph looked at Mary.

"You're right, Son," said Mary finally breaking the silence. "That is a very interesting passage."

Seeing that his Mother was not going to offer any further comment, Jesus decided to change the subject.

"Mother," he asked, "why are you using an old piece of cloth to mend Father's tunic. You have a nice new piece that he bought for you just last week?"

"It isn't wise to do that," replied Mary, smiling as she realized her son was deliberately changing the subject.

"Why not?" persisted Jesus.

"Because that new piece of cloth has not been shrunk yet. When I would wash the tunic again, the new cloth would shrink and tear the old cloth."

"And the damage would be worse than it was before," observed Jesus.

"That's right. So I always use older pieces of cloth that have already shrunk when I patch older garments. It's something my mother taught me," said Mary.

On another evening as Joseph was listening to Jesus read from the scroll of Hosea, he and Mary once again were at a loss as to what to say when Jesus read a passage, stopped and looked at the two of them in silence.

"When Israel was a child," read Jesus moving the wooden pointer carefully from right to left over the words on the scroll, "I loved him, and called my son out of Egypt." (*Hosea 11.1*)

After a few moments of silence, Jesus repeated the question he had asked his parents several months before.

"Dad, why did we move to Egypt when I was a baby and then return to Nazareth a couple years later?"

Joseph could only repeat the same answer they had given earlier.

"When you get a little older, we'll explain everything to you more carefully."

"Jesus," began Mary.

"Yes, I know, Mom. It's time for me to be going to bed."

"You're right," said Mary smiling.

"I'll roll up the scroll first and return it safely to a shelf. 'Night Dad. 'Night, Mom," said Jesus.

Joseph's woodworking shop flourished. His customers could rely on his word when placing orders, and they were most impressed with the careful finishing work given to their orders by Joseph's apprentice, Jesus.

Some customers even seemed to enjoy just stopping in to watch the two at work and to chat casually with Jesus. He was a friendly, alert young boy who was ready to enter into any discussion. He was respectful and had amazing insights for a boy soon to turn seven.

Every so often a customer would come in on some pretext and then, very casually, ask Jesus for an answer to a very serious problem...making believe he was just playing a game with the boy. But when Jesus would give careful consideration to the problem and offer a very valid solution in all seriousness, the customer would be all smiles.

"I have an old sheepdog," said a shepherd who happened to stop by the workshop one day, "who seems to have lost interest in eating. Do you have any suggestions?"

Jesus considered the problem for a while as he continued his work.

"Pet him," said Jesus.

"What?" asked the shepherd.

"If you just spend some time petting your dog before you feed him, he will feel loved and his appetite will return," said Jesus.

"Now, that's a very interesting suggestion for a young boy like you to give. I'll give it a try. Think I'll come to you with all my problems from now on!"

"Dad, may I ask our visitor a question?" said Jesus.

"Would that be alright?" asked Joseph, not wanting to impose on the shepherd in case he needed to leave.

"Why, of course," said the shepherd, flattered that such a wise boy would want to learn something from him.

"Every day," said Jesus, "I watch as you and several other shepherds lead your flocks out to graze in the fields, and then, when you get where you're going, you just let all the sheep mix together and go where they like."

"That's right," said the shepherd. "They are free to graze where they please so long as we keep them all in sight."

"How do you get them all separated again at the end of the day?" asked Jesus.

"Ah, but you see that is no problem at all," said the shepherd. "My sheep know my voice, and the other sheep all know the voices of their own shepherds. All I have to do is call my sheep, and they come running to me."

"That's amazing," said Jesus.

"I know my sheep and they know me," repeated the shepherd.

"Do they all always come or do some get lost sometimes?" asked Jesus.

"Once in a while, if I don't keep a careful eye on them, one will wander off so far that it can no longer hear my voice."

"Then what do you do?" asked Jesus.

"I leave all my other sheep that I have gathered and go look for the one that is lost."

"The lost sheep is that important to you?" asked Jesus.

"Absolutely," said the shepherd.

"It must be very interesting work to be a shepherd," said Jesus.

"And it is. If you like, and you will be allowed, I would be happy to have you come with me into the fields one day to get to know my sheep and see how I work with them."

"I would like that," said Jesus.

"Maybe someday," said Joseph, "but right now you had better finish what you're doing."

After they received whatever advice they came seeking, customers would usually laugh lightheartedly, tell Joseph that that was quite a young boy he had there and turn to leave as though they had just stopped in on a whim…albeit they had come with very real problems and were leaving with solutions they appreciated and valued.

It was an evening late in August after Jesus had turned seven years of age. Jesus had been reading scripture with the other boys under the direction of their synagogue teacher, and once again he had some questions for Joseph.

"Guess what scroll we were reading today, Dad," said Jesus.

"Was it more of Micah or Hosea?" asked Joseph.

"Oh, no," said Jesus. "This time we went way back and began reading Genesis."

"I used to love to hear your grandfather tell Mother and me stories from Genesis," said Mary. "I always thought it was wonderful how all of the different animals got along with each other in the Garden of Eden and how simple and sincere the love was that Adam and Eve had for each other in the very beginning."

"Oh, we got way past that part," said Jesus.

"What part were you reading?" asked Joseph.

"When my turn came, I got to read the verses that say, 'Now the Lord had said to Abraham, Leave your country, and your relatives, and your father's house, and go into a land I will show you. I will help you have many descendents that will become a great nation, and I will bless you, and make your name great; and you will be a blessing,' " (*Genesis 12.1-3*) quoted Jesus verbatim.

Mary and Joseph knew that Jesus was precocious and could read better than most boys his age, but they were always a little surprised when he quoted passages from memory.

"That *is* an interesting passage," said Joseph.

"Dad, didn't you say that we were descendents of Abraham?" asked Jesus.

"Yes, that's true."

"You also said that we were descendents of the tribe of Judah, didn't you?" asked Jesus.

"Why, yes," said Joseph.

"Well," continued Jesus, "just before we were sent home, I heard another boy read another very interesting passage from Genesis."

"What passage was that?" asked Mary, now listening closely to the discussion.

"The staff of authority will not leave Judah, nor his descendents," quoted Jesus from memory, "until Shiloh come; and before him the people will gather." (*Genesis 49.10*)

Joseph and Mary both knew what was going through the nimble brain of her very bright son.

"Teacher said," continued Jesus, "that Shiloh meant the Messiah who would be known for bringing an age of peace to God's people."

Jesus was beginning to figure things out for himself. He was now seven, the age at which most youngsters are believed to enter into what is called the Age of Reason.

Joseph knew it was time.

"Jesus," he said, "do you also remember that I told you that you are a descendent of the house of David?"

"Yes. You said that both you and Mom's mother were both descendents of the House of David, and that I was born in the city of David, Bethlehem."

"Good," said Joseph.

Joseph had been anticipating this evening for a little while and had arranged to borrow several special scrolls from the synagogue to have ready at home.

"Now," he said to Jesus, "bring me the second scroll of Samuel from that shelf. There is something I want you to read to your mother and me."

Jesus carefully read the small leather tags hanging from the ends of several scrolls on the shelf, and quickly returned with the right one. Joseph laid it carefully on the table and began to unroll it until he came to the part he wanted Jesus to read. He then took the small wooden pointer and showed Jesus where to begin.

"And when your life is over," began Jesus, "and you sleep with your ancestors, I will place one of your descendents in charge, and give him a strong kingdom. He will build a house in my name, and I will make the throne of his kingdom last forever. I will be his father, and he will be my son."

As Jesus read on, he paused occasionally to consider the implications of what he read. At each flash of understanding, he would glance up. Finally, he concluded.

"And thy house and thy kingdom shall be established forever before thee: thy throne shall be established forever." (2 Samuel 7.12-16)

When Jesus finished, Joseph carefully re-rolled the scroll and returned it to the shelf himself before sitting back down.

"Do you understand," Joseph finally began, " all of the things that you have read tonight?"

"I understand that God has promised that a leader shall come to Israel who will be a descendent of Abraham, a descendent of the tribe of Judah and a descendent of the house of David."

"You understand correctly," said Mary quietly. "And now, my son, since you are seven years old and can understand things quickly and clearly, Joseph and I have some things we need to share with you that we have kept close to our hearts for many years."

"What are those things, Mother?" asked Jesus.

"Well, you remember all the wonderful things we said happened when you were born in the cave in Bethlehem and what important people came to visit us afterwards, don't you?"

"Yes."

"Well there are many more wonderful things you must know. Joseph and I shall begin to tell them to you. You must listen carefully. If you don't fully understand everything, keep it in your heart and ask God to help you, just as Joseph and I both have had to do."

"Okay, Mother," said Jesus, "I will."

And so Mary began first, telling her son how the angel Gabriel visited her at her mother's house in Nazareth to tell her that she would have a child through the workings of the Holy Spirit and how she was to name that child Jesus.

Then Joseph continued, explaining the message that he had also received from an angel telling him that the child that his fiancée was carrying was the child of the Holy Spirit and that, when it was born, he was to name it Jesus.

"But, Dad," interrupted Jesus. "Does that mean that you are not my father?"

"Joseph loves you like his son," interrupted Mary. "But your true father is in heaven, and Joseph has agreed to take his place here on earth to keep you safe and help you grow into the special role that your father in heaven has planned for you."

The conversation went on well into the night as Joseph paused occasionally, and asked Jesus to get more wood to throw on the their small fire while he and Mary quietly discussed what they would share next.

Mary then told her son about the wonderful birth of his cousin that she had learned had been named John by his parents Joachim and Elizabeth.

And Joseph told Jesus about the amazing things that were said to them at the time of his presentation in the Temple in Jerusalem by the old man named Simeon and the aged widow named Anna.

After Jesus listened carefully and thoughtfully to everything that his mother and Joseph told him, he sat quietly for a while.

Although it was now very late, none of them was tired. This was a moment to which Mary and Joseph had looked forward for years, and the mind of Jesus was racing as he carefully considered all the information being shared with him.

"And so," Jesus said after a long silence, "why did we travel to Egypt after I was born?"

Joseph reminded Jesus about Micah's prophecy that the now-dead King Herod had discovered about a king of Israel who would be born in Bethlehem, and explained how the three Magi who had visited them two years later had been warned in a dream not to return to Jerusalem to tell King Herod where they had found them and how he himself had been visited again by an angel who warned him to flee immediately with his wife and her child into Egypt to save the child's life.

"And what made you decide to return to Nazareth?" asked Jesus.

"As promised," said Joseph. "the same angel came back to let me know that King Herod had died, and that it would now be safe for us to return to your mother's hometown. And we have been here ever since."

"You realize, my son," said Mary, "that the things we have told you tonight are very special. They are secrets shared with us by angels of our Father in Heaven, and we have carefully guarded them over the years. You, too, must continue to guard them as you pray and ask your Father in Heaven to show you what they all mean."

"I'll be very careful, Mother."

"Especially," said Joseph, "when you are studying scripture with the other boys. You must be careful not to give them reasons to believe that you think you are better than they are. God will let you know when he wants you to begin to share these secrets with others. To tell them to anyone before that time will only incite envy and hatred. Just realize that your mother and I believe that you are the Immanuel that the prophet Isaiah predicted would be born to a young maiden from the house of David. Only when you get older will you come to realize what the will of your Father in Heaven is for you as his Son on earth. Until then you must pray and study and carefully ponder all these things in your heart as your mother and I have done these past years."

Again, there was a long silence as a sort of peace filled the room and the fire slowly died down.

"And now," said Mary.

"I know," said Jesus, "It's time for this young boy to go to bed."

"Good night, son," said Mary. "Love you."

"Love you both," said Jesus as he headed for his cot.

Chapter 4

Jesus as a Teenager

"Are we all ready?" asked Joseph.

"Son," said Mary, "if you will grab the food basket from the table and secure it to the ass, I believe everything else is already packed."

"Yes, Mother. I've already tied our other bundles to the saddle, so this should do it."

"Come, Mary," said Joseph, "and I'll help you up. I will walk ahead, and your son will walk along side in case you need anything."

And so the family was soon on the road through Perea once again, joining many other families already making the 100-mile trip south toward Jerusalem for the annual Passover visit to the Temple. They would not rush. Joseph intended to travel only about twenty miles each day.

They had made the trip annually since their return to Nazareth from Egypt, and each year Jesus looked forward more eagerly to his visit to the great Temple. He was now twelve years old and could hardly wait to enter into discussions with other students and with whatever teachers might have time to spend with the young boys eager to show off their familiarity with the scriptures.

Jesus had spent many days during his twelfth year in intense discussions at the house that served as their synagogue in Nazareth. He was already very familiar with all of the texts and was beginning to analyze and interpret the writings according to his own thinking—having by now accepted the fact that he had a very special role to play (albeit a still secret one)—as the Son of God on earth. He had been thinking and discussing a lot about the Kingdom of God in Heaven, but more especially about how it was meant to exist among God's people on earth. He had held many discussions trying to convince others at the synagogue of the necessity of praising the name of God everyday through personal prayer and not just through public sacrifices. When he got to the Temple in Jerusalem he intended to take his discussions to a new level. He wanted to try and convince others of the need to place total reliance on God for their daily necessities—just as those who were led by Moses came to rely on God for their daily supply of manna in the dessert. He would see where the discussion would go from there.

Each night all the travelers would make camp along side the road, some setting up small tents, others placing sleeping mats next to open fires. Open fires meant relaxation and, what Jesus enjoyed most, they also meant stories shared with fellow travelers. Jesus was always eager to hear a new story, especially one that taught a lesson or carried a special message. The variety of stories seemed to be endless, and Jesus wanted to hear them all.

"When we enter Jerusalem," said Joseph one night as his family was preparing to go to sleep, "we must be sure and stay together. There will be hundreds of people in the streets and around the Temple."

"Should I stay with you and Mother at all times, or can I spend time with some of the friends I have made during the trip?" asked Jesus.

"Oh," asked Mary, "don't you think it would be alright for him to spend time with his young friends so long as they all stay among familiar faces?"

"That would probably be alright," said Joseph.

"Mother," said Jesus, "I would especially like to be able to join students who might be holding discussions with teachers and Rabbis in the Temple while we are there."

"That will be fine, Son. Just be aware when it is time for us to leave so that Joseph doesn't have to come looking for you."

When Jesus finally got his chance to join a group of students at the great Temple, he patiently waited his turn to speak. When it came, he bravely shared the thoughts he had been working on at the synagogue in Nazareth.

"Would everyone agree that private prayer can be as effective as public sacrifices?" asked Jesus.

"That may be true," said a teacher who had agreed to meet with the boys, "but the laws of Moses also require certain public sacrifices to be offered to God."

"Yes, but I believe that God's name should be praised daily by everyone, and not everyone has the time or the coins to make public sacrifices to God everyday," said Jesus.

After Jesus cleverly turned the discussion to the Kingdom of God, he began to present some of the other ideas on which he had been working.

"We all know that the Kingdom of God is in Heaven, but I wonder what you all think the Kingdom of God should be like here among His people on earth?" asked Jesus.

The discussion quickly grew hot and heavy, with some suggesting that God's Kingdom among His people would involve royal families, palaces and armies. After all had had a chance to share their ideas, Jesus calmly presented his own view.

"I believe that the Kingdom of God should exist within His people, and not be an external government of His people," suggested Jesus.

This novel idea was met with frowns and silence.

"I believe that the Kingdom of God," continued Jesus, "should be shown through the actions of His people, by the way they live their daily lives, by how they treat each other. I believe that those who live in the Kingdom of God on earth should try not to hurt each other and yet always be ready to forgive those who may hurt them. I believe that if God's people want to experience His Kingdom in their daily lives, they need to rely on Him totally. They need to ask His help in avoiding situations that will cause them to do wrong and in avoiding dangers and hardships that might otherwise come their way."

"That is a very interesting idea that the young man from Nazareth is suggesting," said the teacher. "He has obviously given it a great deal of thought."

"And what prayer would you suggest we pray each day to ask for all this help?" asked the teacher."

"It could be a very simple one," said Jesus.

"For example?" asked the teacher, pressing his point.

"Well, for instance," said Jesus. "It could go something like this: Our Father in Heaven, holy is Your name. May Your kingdom come, and Your will be done, here among Your people as it is in Heaven. Give us the bread we will need for our daily food, and forgive us all that we have done wrong just as we forgive those who wrong us. And please don't allow us to be put to the test, but protect us from evil."

"And that's it?" asked another of the students.

"It could be just that short and simple," said Jesus. "And each person could say the prayer privately as often as he wanted to. I'm personally convinced that our Father in Heaven hears all the prayers we say privately, or publicly, and that He will help all who pray to Him."

This was, of course, followed by a considerable amount of discussion—especially since some students were unwilling to accept the custom of the elitist Pharisees of addressing God as "Father." In the end, Jesus agreed that he would return the next day to defend his suggestions.

By the next day, however, Joseph and Mary, and the other travelers from Nazareth, had completed their annual offerings and Passover rituals and had packed up to begin their return trip home.

Mary was not concerned when she did not see her son on the road during the day since she and Joseph had given him permission to travel in the company of his friends. But when he didn't show up at their campfire in the evening, she began to get a little worried.

"Joseph, have you seen Jesus today?" asked Mary.

"No, but I'm sure he's with his friends as we told him he could be," said Joseph, who then went about his business tending their small campfire and preparing their sleeping mats.

"Well, I think you should go look for him if he doesn't show up by the time I have our dinner ready."

Joseph said that he would.

Unfortunately, Jesus could be found nowhere, and none of his friends was sure what had happened to him. It was late in the evening before Joseph was able to return to Mary.

"Your son is nowhere among our fellow travelers," said Joseph, using a defensive note frequently used by spouses when they are tired.

"What should we do?" asked Mary.

"Well, there's not a lot we can do this late at night, but I think that you and I should return to Jerusalem early tomorrow morning to look for him."

And so, the next morning, as all the other travelers packed their belongings and loaded their packs and food onto their animals, Joseph led the ass that carried Mary and their belongings back toward Jerusalem.

Neither Joseph nor Mary spoke much during the day. Their pace was slow since they were fighting traffic. Most travelers were leaving Jerusalem instead of heading toward the town. More than once, Joseph had to lead the ass off to the side of the road to allow a wagon or cart to pass. Occasionally, even tight clusters of people traveling on foot would refuse to make room for them, and once again Mary and he would find themselves waiting off to the side until the group passed.

About midday, Mary finally broke their silence.

"I pray that he has come to no harm," said Mary.

"Oh, I'm sure he's alright. Knowing him, he's probably either listening to stories at a public well or discussing scriptures with a group at the great Temple," suggested Joseph.

"I hope you're right," said Mary. "Jerusalem is no place for a twelve-year old boy to be wandering about on his own."

It took Joseph and Mary the entire day just to reach the outskirts of Jerusalem.

"We'll set up our camp here close to the city wall," said Joseph as he helped Mary down from their ass. "In the morning we'll begin our search in the city."

After spending most of the third day asking around at the various public wells and other places where young people seemed to gather, they finally made their way back to the great Temple. As Mary remained with their animal and their belongings outside the Temple precinct, Joseph began to look into each of the small discussion rooms that abounded on the different levels of the building. And before too long, he heard the gentle but firm voice of Jesus holding forth in one of the rooms.

"I'm not saying that the commands of the law are to be overlooked. My point is that if the people of God would only be motivated by the love of God and the love for each other, we would see that love can ask far more from God's people than fear can command."

"Jesus," said Joseph standing in the doorway and using his most authoritative adult voice.

"Dad," said Jesus, turning abruptly. "Is it time for us to leave?"

"Yes," said Joseph not wanting to embarrass Jesus before the other students. "Your Mother and I are waiting."

Jesus gathered up his things and excused himself from the group.

"Will we see you again next year?" called out one of the young boys with whom Jesus had been talking.

"You can count on it," said Jesus. "We'll continue our discussion then."

As he prepared to follow Joseph, the Rabbi in charge of the group spoke up.

"Before you leave, young man, I would like a word with you."

Jesus paused and waited for the Rabbi to come to the door. In the privacy of the hallway, the Rabbi spoke.

"Your name is Jesus, right?" asked the Rabbi.

"Yes, Sir. Jesus from Nazareth."

"When you return next year, I would need to have a long talk with you before you will be allowed to enter into discussions with the other boys. Is that understood?"

"Yes, Sir," said Jesus. "It will be an honor to speak with you individually."

Jesus walked in silence with Joseph until they left the main door of the Temple and approached Mary.

"Hi, Mother," said Jesus when he drew near to her. "Are we ready to leave?"

"Son, we began our trip back home three days ago. When we saw that you did not join us at our fire on the evening of our first day, Joseph searched for you among your friends in our traveling group."

"That's when we decided to return to Jerusalem to look for you, young man," said Joseph.

"Son," said Mary, "why have you done this to us? Joseph and I were very worried about you."

"You've caused your mother a great deal of grief," emphasized Joseph.

"I'm sorry if I worried you and made you sad, but really you shouldn't have been overly concerned about me," said Jesus.

"And why not?" asked Mary.

"Don't you realize that I must be about my Father's business," said Jesus, speaking respectfully yet firmly as he looked them both in the eye.

Neither Joseph nor Mary replied. Although at the time they did not fully understand exactly what Jesus meant, he said it in such a way that they believed he knew what he was talking about and should not be questioned further.

Jesus, however, was very careful after that not to give either his mother or Joseph any cause for concern over his safety.

Mary, as was her custom regarding her amazing son, kept all these things in her heart as she watched him grow into a tall young man and increase in wisdom and favor both with man and God.

Over the course of the next few years, Jesus continued his study and discussions of the scripture with other students at the synagogue in Nazareth, and every year he presented his newly refined ideas and conclusions to those whom he would see at the great Temple during the family's annual Passover trip to Jerusalem.

Jesus spent his eighteenth year focusing on the Psalms of David, especially on those that seemed to indicate the people that David considered to be "blessed."

"Blessed is the man who delights in the law of the Lord." (*1.1-2*)

"Blessed are those who remember judgment and act correctly." (*106.3*)

"Blessed is the man who fears the Lord and delights in his commandments." (*112.1*)

"Blessed are the undefeated who walk in the law of the Lord." (*119.1*)

"Are these really the most important indications that a man is blessed?" Jesus would ask his fellow students and their teacher in the synagogue in Nazareth.

"Don't you think they are?" others would question.

"Well, don't take this the wrong way, but I think that, incorrectly understood, the laws of Moses can be a little harsh."

"So are you putting down the laws of Moses?" asked a teacher.

"No, I'm not putting them down. But I do think we need to study them more carefully so we can understand the real intentions of God's laws."

"What real intentions?" asked a fellow student.

"Well, for one thing, I believe the emphasis should be on the moral lives of God's people, and how they show their love to God and to each other, rather than placing all the emphasis on sacrifices and religious ceremonies that can often be impersonal."

"So what kind of improvements and changes would you suggest?" asked a visiting Rabbi who had happened to stop by and was listening to the discussion.

"Well," said Jesus, softening his tone out of respect for the Rabbi, "I'm still thinking it all through, but somehow I believe that God's people need a new spirit, one that just doesn't emphasize strict observance of external rules and regulations. I think the old moral order based on the strict application of the laws of Moses has to be given a new life, a new spirit."

"What kind of new spirit?" insisted the Rabbi.

"The new spirit I'm thinking of should be gentle, generous, and simple, yet sincere, prudent, and, above all, energetic. I think God's people need to try to reflect their perfect Father in Heaven in their daily lives."

"And just what is going to drive this new spirit?" asked a teacher.

"Love," replied Jesus. "As far as I have been able to determine, all of the Mosaic laws can be simplified into two simple statements based on love."

"What two simple statements?" asked a student.

"Love God the Father with all your heart, soul and mind, and love your neighbor as yourself."

"It sounds like you've been talking with the Pharisees," said the Rabbi, who recognized one of the main tenets of that Holier than Thou group in Jesus' statement.

"I'm familiar with their teachings," said Jesus.

Jesus knew that his ideas would not be immediately accepted by those who were listening to him, but he would keep thinking them through and explaining them and discussing them. In the end, he felt confident that he would be able to state his new ideas in a way that would win the hearts of his listeners and inspire them to begin living new lives with a new spirit. A spirit based more on love than on fear.

Jesus also knew that he wanted to rethink David's examples of who should be considered blessed. The emphasis should not be so much on those who adhere strictly to the laws of God out of fear. He would just have to come up with his own list of people that should be considered "blessed" in the eyes of his Father in Heaven.

By the time Jesus was nineteen years old, not only was he a very accomplished carpenter, but he had also spent countless hours studying all of the scriptures. He had prayed to his Father in Heaven for guidance and insight into His words as revealed through the prophets. He had shared and tried to explain his new understanding of his Father's will to his fellow students at the synagogue in Nazareth and at the Temple in Jerusalem.

While the ideas of Jesus did spark new hope and life in many of his fellow students, Rabbis began to be suspicious of this young man who was challenging years of Mosaic teaching and traditions. Some even thought they picked up on subtle hints that this young man named Jesus might even consider himself to be the Messiah whose arrival was foretold by the prophets, especially Isaiah. But this idea seemed so dangerously radical that they thought for sure that they had misheard or misinterpreted the things the young man had said.

Jesus was indeed very absorbed in the study of the Messianic prophecies during his nineteenth year. He had privately discussed all of the early references with his mother and Joseph. The three of them had spent many evenings discussing Jeremiah's references to the killing of infants (*31.15*) that would accompany the birth of the Messiah. The writings of Isaiah held a wealth of references to how the Messiah would be anointed by the Holy Spirit (*11.2*), would be heralded by a messenger of the Lord, would perform miracles (*35.5-6*), would, while living in Galilee, bring God's people a new interpretation of the scriptures that would be good news to their ears and their lives. (*9.1*)

Joseph and Mary both agreed that all of these writings definitely pointed to the fact that Jesus was indeed the Messiah that had been promised, the Immanuel that Isaiah wrote would be born of a young maiden, the Son of God, the one that the Lord God would place on the throne of David to be the Savior of His people.

During this, his nineteenth year, however, Jesus had also studied, even more carefully, the rest of the Messianic prophecies, ones he did not wish to discuss with his Mother or Joseph because he knew they would only upset and worry them.

In the writings of Malachi (*3.1*), Jesus read how, as God's messenger, he was destined to come to His Temple as Lord and correct the wrongs that he would see there. In Zechariah (*9.9*) he read how he was destined to be proclaimed King as he would enter Jerusalem riding an ass. From a psalm of David (*118.22*) he realized that before becoming the headstone of God's people, he would be rejected by them.

Jesus knew that he would have to keep to himself all the terrible prophecies foretelling the insults and torture that he was destined to endure as recorded in other psalms (*22, 34.20, 41.9, 69,21*), and in the writings of Zechariah (*11.12, 12.10*) and Isaiah (*53*). These trials that he would have to endure for his Father as the Messiah he would keep to himself until the time came to share them with those who needed to know.

But from the Psalms (*16.10*) Jesus also learned that his Father would not allow his Holy One to die or to suffer corruption after being crucified with thieves as predicted by Isaiah. Ezechiel (37.13) and Hosea (6.1-2; *13.14*) had prophesied that his father would raise him up and the Psalms of David (*68.18, 110.1*) assured Jesus that, as God among men, Immanuel, he would eventually ascend on high and sit at the right hand of his Father in Heaven.

Jesus had learned from the prophecies, and chose not to share with Mary and Joseph, the pain he would have to suffer on behalf of God's people, but he also knew that his Father in Heaven would be with him as he embraced his role as the savior of His people.

Chapter 5

Jesus Begins Ten Years of Travel

By the time Jesus was 20 years old, he had mastered all that he was intended to learn from the prophets of his Father in Heaven. He understood clearly his role as Messiah to the people of God, and had almost completely worked out the messages and new spirit that he believed his Father in Heaven wished him to share with His people as well as with the Gentiles and perhaps even with the lost tribes of Israel. Jesus, however, was not yet ready to begin his public life and move toward the final fulfillments of the Messianic prophecies.

Jesus determined that he needed some time to travel. He needed to learn what beliefs were held by those who lived in other lands, and to learn how they were living the lives that had been given them by his Father in Heaven.

And so, one day, Jesus decided to explain his plans to his mother and Joseph.

"Joseph," he began. "do you believe it would be possible for you to run your carpentry shop on your own and continue to provide for Mother's care if I no longer worked beside you?"

"Oh, I think so," said Joseph, smiling. "Don't forget, young man, that I taught you everything you know about carpentry."

"Yes, I know. But I'm wondering if it would be a great hardship on you to handle all the orders on your own for a while?"

"Well, you know that you are a great help to me. It would be an adjustment if you were to leave, but I think I could handle it. Why do you ask?"

"Well," began Jesus as diplomatically as possible, "now that I am 20 years old, I believe it is the will of my Father in Heaven that I travel beyond the borders of Judea and visit and get to know those people who live in the far reaches of His Kingdom on earth. I believe there are many things that I can learn from them."

"But, Son," interrupted Mary, "what about the role our Father in Heaven wants you to play here as the Messiah to the people of Israel?"

"Mother," began Jesus, "although I'm 20 years old, I am not yet ready to reveal myself to God's people as their Messiah. I believe that this decision is the will of my Father in Heaven."

"Exactly where do you intend to go?" asked Joseph.

"Well, first of all, I would like to revisit Egypt where we lived for a while after I was born. I understand there are some very wise and clever men in Alexandria," said Jesus.

"You do realize that Alexandria is at least 400 miles from here, don't you?" questioned Joseph.

"Yes, I do," said Jesus. "It will be a long walk, but I will pass the time talking with those I meet on the road and getting to know those who offer me hospitality in the evenings. Everyone has a story, and you know how I love to hear stories."

"And where will you go after that?' asked Mary.

"Then," said Jesus, "I would like to travel to the land from which the Magi came to visit us in Bethlehem. I would like to meet other Magi who may be living there and learn what wisdom they have acquired through their studies."

"Will you then return home?" asked Joseph.

"Before I return to Nazareth, I intend to travel as the Holy Spirit of my Father indicates and to visit those lands where the wisest and most holy of men are said to live and study. But, to put your minds at ease, it is my intention to return to Nazareth before ten years have passed."

"Ten years?" asked Mary, a little surprised.

"Yes, Mother. For the Holy Spirit has revealed to me that it will be when I am 30 years old that I am to begin my work with the people of Israel and begin to share with them a new spirit of the laws of Moses and the Good News that I have for them as their Messiah."

"What good news?" asked Joseph.

"My Good News will reveal how their Father in Heaven loves them and wants them to love each other. No longer will they need to live in fear and oppression. The Good News will be that the time for the Kingdom of God on earth has come, and that this Kingdom is to exist in them, in their minds and in their hearts. The Good News will be that the Kingdom of God will not be run by kings with palaces and armies but will exist in the actions of God's people toward Him and toward each other."

"What you are saying could be viewed as very radical. Do you think your message will be welcomed by God's people?" asked Joseph.

"Not at first," continued Jesus. "I will, no doubt, be viewed as a threat to both the political and religious leaders in Judea. But I believe that this will be my role as the Messiah. While my long-range plan is to bring peace to God's people, I'm afraid that I will at first introduce strife as people are forced to re-evaluate the old moral, legalistic Mosaic codes and come to accept a new moral code based on a gentle, generous and sincere spirit, a spirit inspired solely by love for the Father in Heaven and for each other."

"But you would be upsetting the harmony of families who have based their lives on the moral code of Moses for generations," observed Mary.

"Family members will no doubt be set against each other. Whole families will become opposed to each other, and whole communities will be thrown into conflict over my Good News before they finally come to accept it. But in the end, God's message will be delivered, and those that have ears to hear will receive it."

"But, my son," objected Mary, "don't you think such a task should be undertaken slowly and carried on over a great number of years? You don't want to make people hate you by rushing them, do you?"

"Mother," answered Jesus, "one of the main reasons I want to travel at this time is that I don't think I will have a great number of years to perform my task once I reveal myself as the Messiah to God's people. I will need to be as ready as possible. I will need to have it very clear in my own mind what I am going to do. I want to learn to be as effective as possible in getting people to listen to me and accept my message. The Salvation of God's people will depend on how well I fill my role as the Messiah. And not to upset you, Mother, but I'm afraid that there will be those who will hate me and may even wish to put me to death."

"Do you believe that this is the will of your Father in Heaven?" asked Joseph.

"Yes, I do."

"Do you believe that after ten years you will be ready?" asked Mary.

"Yes, Mother. I do. And that is when I shall return here to Nazareth to begin my public life as the Messiah."

"I don't have a lot of silver to offer you for your travels," said Joseph, always practical.

"My Father in Heaven who looks after the birds of the sky and the flowers of the fields will provide all that I need on my travels. I will go where I am welcome, eat what is offered, wear what is given me, and sleep where a mat is provided. As I am the Son of God among both Jews and Gentiles, His people will provide all that I need."

The next morning, Jesus was up early. He brought his mother a fresh bucket of water from the well and then prepared to leave.

"But why don't you let me pack you some figs and a loaf of bread to take with you? Joseph, get one of the small wine skins for him!" said Mary.

"Mother, I'll be fine. Trust me. I've put my faith in my Father in Heaven."

"Well, be careful," said Joseph. "The roads aren't always safe. A person hears many stories these days."

"And stop to rest once in a while, especially during the hottest part of the day," encouraged Mary.

"Don't worry, Mom. I'll be just fine. May the peace of my Father in Heaven be with both of you and may his angels protect you."

And so Jesus began his ten-year journey during which he would continue to prepare himself for his role as the Messiah to the people of Israel and to all of God's people.

He decided to travel the road that ran along the Jordan River to Jericho. Occasionally, he would be joined by other travelers who would walk with him for several miles and help pass the time in conversation. Mostly, however, he walked alone and enjoyed having the time to observe nature and consider all that he had studied and been told of what was to be expected of him.

After passing through Jericho and spending several nights camping along side the road, Jesus finally approached an inn located half way between Jericho and Jerusalem. As he drew near, the innkeeper happened to be sitting on a bench in the shade. The man called out to Jesus.

"Traveler, you look warm. Won't you come and rest and have something to drink?"

Jesus accepted the invitation, and the two were soon engaged in friendly conversation.

The innkeeper took an immediate liking to Jesus, and when he learned of the long trip he had ahead of him, he offered him a meal and a place to sleep at no charge.

Later that evening, Jesus noticed the wife of the innkeeper taking a small tray of food and fresh bandages into one of the guest rooms.

"Is someone hurt?" asked Jesus.

"Yes," said the innkeeper. "It is a traveler who was coming from Jerusalem on his way to Jericho."

"What happened to him?" asked Jesus.

"Perhaps you would like to ask him," said the innkeeper. "He will probably appreciate your company."

Jesus waited for the innkeeper's wife to finish changing the injured man's bandages and then quietly entered his room and sat down on a small stool next to the bed. When the injured man opened his eyes to look at him, Jesus asked him if he would like a sip of water.

"Please," said the injured man.

"May I ask what happened to you?" asked Jesus.

"Well," said the injured man, "my mouth is still a little swollen so it may be hard for you to understand me."

"That's alright. Just take your time. I think I'll be able to understand you just fine," encouraged Jesus.

"Well," began the injured man, "do you know the road that runs between Jerusalem and Jericho?"

"Yes," said Jesus, "I recently passed through Jericho."

"Well, it was just after midday, and I was on that road making my way to Jericho when I was attacked by a gang of robbers."

"Before I left my home," said Jesus, "I was warned that it's getting very dangerous to travel these days."

"Let me tell you," said the injured man. "Not only did they take my money, they even stripped off my clothes and then beat me half to death."

"Who came to your aid?" asked Jesus.

"Well, that's a whole story in itself. One you might not even believe."

"Try me," said Jesus.

"Well, I must have been knocked unconscious because when I finally realized what had happened to me, it was just starting to get dark. I tried to drag myself out of the ditch where they had thrown me, but I could hardly move."

"Did you call out for help?" asked Jesus.

"As soon as I saw someone coming, I did. It was a priest, and I thought for sure that he would help me."

"Did he?"

"I couldn't even get him to look at me although I shouted as loud as I could. In fact, he made of point of crossing over to the other side of the road so he wouldn't have to look at me."

"A priest, you say?" asked Jesus.

"Yes, I could tell by his vest. By then I was really starting to hurt so I laid my head down and tried to catch my breath for awhile."

"Then what happened?"

"The next time I looked up, I saw a man who seemed to be in his thirties. When he got closer, I saw that he was wearing the sash of a temple helper, a Levite. I know he saw me because he got this real disgusted look on his face. I begged him to help me because I had been attacked by robbers."

"What did he do?"

"He made believe he didn't hear me and crossed over to the far side of the road too. Maybe he thought I might get up and chase him or something."

"So, how did you get here?" asked Jesus.

"Well, by then I had pretty much given up hope. But just before it got completely dark, I suddenly became aware that a man was kneeling down next to me in the ditch. I noticed he was wearing one of those flat topped round hats that Samaritans wear. And you know what they say about Samaritans. I figured he was probably checking to see if there was anything left that he could steal. I was surprised when he asked if I could stand up. With his help, we made it back up on the road where he set me down while he got some oil and wine out of a pack strapped to the side of a pack animal he had with him. He gently washed the dirt from my wounds. Then he took a clean cloth and began to tear it in strips."

"So was he the one who wrapped your ribs and your arms and legs?" asked Jesus.

"And he did a pretty good job. When he was done, he helped me stand up again and carefully lifted me up onto the back of his pack animal."

"And he brought him here," said the innkeeper who had been standing in the doorway listening.

"A Samaritan?" asked Jesus.

"Yes, and a very generous one," added the innkeeper. "Before he left the next day, he gave me two silver coins and told me to take care of this gentleman. He even said that if I had to spend more than two silver coins on his care, he would pay the difference when he passed this way again."

"Now that was a true neighbor," said Jesus. "Blessed are men like that who show mercy, for they will have mercy shown to them."

"He was definitely a true neighbor," said the injured man, "and I hope that he will indeed have mercy shown to him in his time of need."

"Here," said Jesus, "let me get you another sip of water, and then you had better try to get some rest so you can get well."

Before continuing his journey toward Jerusalem in the morning, Jesus stopped by the injured man's room to wish him well.

"May the peace of our Father in Heaven be with you as you recover," said Jesus.

"And also with you, my friend."

"You should know," comforted Jesus, "that in the eyes of our Father in Heaven, you are blessed for your patient endurance of your suffering. The comfort you receive from Him will exceed your current sorrow."

Jesus thanked the innkeeper for his hospitality and praised him for the kind and gentle care that he and his wife were offering the injured man. He then took his leave.

When Jesus was passing through Jerusalem, he decided to stop at the great Temple to ask his Father in Heaven to watch over him on his long journey. If there were bandits out there who were willing to beat travelers almost to death for a few coins and their clothing, he would need all the help he could get.

At the Temple Jesus was shocked to see how disrespectfully the vendors were doing business even within the Temple precinct. Moneychangers were making so much noise right outside the doors of the Temple that it was hard for those who wanted to pray to concentrate. He knew this was not right, and, when the time came, he knew he would have to let them all know just how wrong it was.

Today, however, would not be the day.

As Jesus entered the Temple, he noticed that there were two other men already inside praying. One man, a Pharisee stood proudly thanking God that he was not like other men with whom he dealt.

"Oh, God," prayed the Pharisee in a low, but audible voice, "I thank you for making me a just man. I thank you that I am not an adulterer and that I do not extort money wrongfully from others like that tax collector lurking in the back of your Temple. All my friends and family know that I fast twice a week, and I let everyone know that I freely tithe ten percent of all that I possess. For all this I thank you."

Jesus finally tuned the Pharisee out and concentrated on his own silent prayers.

On his way out of the Temple, Jesus noticed the tax collector whom the Pharisee had mentioned. The poor man was huddled over, leaning against the back wall, striking his breast. As Jesus passed him on the way to the door, he overheard the poor man's humble prayer.

"God, be merciful to me a sinner! God, be merciful to me a sinner! God, be merciful to me a sinner."

Jesus would have liked to have gone up to the poor man and consoled him, assuring him that his humble prayer was, indeed, being heard by God, and that he should feel free to go in peace. His time for public action, however, had not yet come.

As he left the Temple, Jesus thought to himself, "Blessed are men like that who have lowly views of themselves, who are poor in spirit. They may not realize it, but the Kingdom of Heaven will be theirs."

About four days south of Jerusalem, Jesus happened to come to a little house located outside of a small provincial town. As he drew near, he could see a frail old woman dressed in unbleached, gray-colored clothing bustling about, broom in hand.

Jesus approached nearer and saw that the poor old woman seemed to be nearly frantic.

"Peace be with you, Ma'am," said Jesus, hoping to offer her a bit of comfort. "Is something wrong? Is there something I can help you with?"

"I've lost it! I've lost it," said the old woman.

"What have you lost?" asked Jesus.

The old woman stopped, turned and gave Jesus a very deliberate look.

"What have I lost?"

"Yes, Ma'am. What have you lost?" repeated Jesus.

"Can't you see I'm a widow? I've lost my husband. Then I lost the money that is owed me by my neighbor who bought the rights to a small pasture that used to belong to my husband. The man refuses to pay, and I can't get the provincial judge to listen to my side of the story. And now, to top it all off, I've lost one of the last ten drachmas that I have to my name. You ask what I have lost? Well, that's what I have lost."

Jesus was almost beginning to feel sorry for having bothered the widow, but he felt that she deserved to be comforted.

"Is there anything I can do?" asked Jesus.

"Well," said the widow, feeling the calming effect of her visitor's words, "you can come in and rest for a while. I don't have much to offer, but you can have a little something to eat while I keep looking around."

Jesus accepted the widow's invitation and bent to enter the low doorway of her house. He sat in the only chair available and waited as his hostess placed a cup of water and some bread and cheese before him.

"So, the judge won't hear your complaint against your neighbor?" asked Jesus.

"That's right. Every week I walk into town and get in line with others who have complaints for him to hear, and he always refuses to listen to what I have to say."

"Is your neighbor an influential man in the community?" asked Jesus.

"He probably is. And I'm just a poor widow. But, let me tell you, I'm not going to give up. It's not right the way I'm being treated, and I'll keep bothering that judge for the next ten years if I have to."

Jesus finished his food and drink before standing to leave.

"I thank you for your kindness," said Jesus. "I hope you find your lost coin, and don't give up on the judge. Sooner or later he's bound to come around."

As Jesus walked away from the widow's small house, he thought to himself, "Blessed are people like this poor widow who hunger for justice. They will surely have their fill."

Several days later, as Jesus was passing the walls of a very wealthy estate, he heard the cries of man who was being tortured. Jesus walked to the nearest gate where he was met by a gatekeeper.

"And what is your business here?" asked the gatekeeper.

"I couldn't help but hear the cries of a man being tortured," said Jesus, "and I would like to intercede on his behalf if I could."

"And who are you?" asked the gatekeeper.

"My name is Jesus. I am traveling from the town of Nazareth to Alexandria as I prepare to do the will of my Father in Heaven."

Something about the countenance of Jesus and the sincerity of his words made the gatekeeper decide to respect his request.

"If you wish to intercede, you will need to speak to the master of the estate," said the gatekeeper.

"That I will gladly do," said Jesus.

The gatekeeper called to another servant standing nearby and gave him instructions to take Jesus to see the master.

When Jesus was presented to the master of the estate, this man, too, was taken by the calm countenance of his visitor. He thought he sensed a certain bearing that commanded respect, but he couldn't exactly put his finger on what it was.

"Bring us a tray of food and some drink," ordered the master.

Once Jesus had accepted a seat and reintroduced himself, he asked about the man being tortured.

"Well, Sir," began the master, "I am not, by nature, a harsh man. In fact, I try to go out of my way to give people a break whenever I can. That man, however, deserves no mercy."

"And why is that?" asked Jesus.

"The man whose cries of pain you heard was once one of my head servants. I trusted him. Whenever he needed extra money for his family, I gladly loaned it to him on his word that he would pay it all back when requested."

"How much did you end up loaning him?" asked Jesus.

"Ten thousand silver coins."

"You trusted him very much, didn't you?" said Jesus, smiling.

"Indeed I did. He was a good servant and one whom I had put in charge of many other servants. At least until the day I told him that it was time to repay what he owed."

"What happened that day?" asked Jesus.

"When I called him into my office and explained that I now needed to have his loan repaid, he calmly announced that he had nothing on hand with which to repay it. I tried to make him understand that the payment was urgently needed for another investment, and that he would have to come up with it one way or another. Of course, he continued to insist he had no way at all to make the payment."

"Then what happened?" asked Jesus.

"Well, he left me no choice. Since I was anxious to have the funds to make my new investment, I told him that I would have to sell him, his wife and his family into slavery."

"I'm sure that was a hard decision" said Jesus. "How did he take it?"

"Not well. He threw himself at my feet and, looking up at me with tears in his eyes, begged for mercy. He promised that if I just gave him a little time, he would pay it all back."

"Did you agree to give him more time?"

"Actually, I was so moved by his tears and by my fondness for his family that I told him just to forget about it."

"You forgave his loan?"

"Every coin of it. Suddenly, my planned investment just didn't seem as important to me as it did originally. I told him he could go, but that he should think twice about coming to me for loans in the future."

"So why are you having him tortured?" asked Jesus.

"Let me tell you why," said the master of the estate. "No sooner did he leave my office than he happened to come across one of the servants who worked under him to whom he had loaned a mere one hundred silver coins. Those who saw it happen say that he grabbed the man and strangled him saying he would have him thrown into prison if he didn't repay what he owed immediately."

"Did the man pay him?"

"No. And that's just it. That servant also fell to his knees and begged for mercy, insisting that he would pay him back as soon as he could."

"So, I take it your servant did not forgive the man his debt of one hundred silver coins," said Jesus.

"No he didn't. In fact, by the time I heard about it, the poor man had been thrown into prison without even having been given a chance to see his wife and children."

"He certainly didn't share your compassion, did he?" said Jesus.

"Absolutely not. As soon as I heard about it, I had him brought before me and I let him know exactly what I thought about him. As far as I'm concerned, the man will be tortured until every last silver coin is paid back."

"May I ask a favor?" said Jesus.

"That will depend on what it is," replied the master cautiously.

"May I visit the man you are torturing before I leave your estate?"

"If you wish," said the master. "But may I ask why?"

"Every man," said Jesus, "deserves compassion, no matter what wrong he has done. I would like a chance to comfort him and encourage him to bear with a proper spirit the punishment he seems rightly to deserve."

As Jesus left the estate, the grounds were quiet. The day's torture had been completed.

It was very sad. Jesus felt sorry for all of them and for the situation into which they had gotten themselves.

Chapter 6

Jesus in Alexandria

A large crowd was gathered outside a small Egyptian temple dedicated to Sekhmet, a goddess of healing. What had begun as a simple demonstration of magic had quickly captured the minds of the spectators.

In between tricks, a priest of the temple took advantage of the attention being given him by the crowd to preach and teach his religious truths and precepts. Each time their attention would seem to waver or it was noticed that some spectators were beginning to walk off, a greater and even more impressive feat of magic would be performed.

"Do you see the staff which the priest holds in his hand?" said the priest's deacon in a commanding voice.

"Yes, we see it," shouted one of the spectators.

"If there are any of you who doubt the powers of this great priest," said the deacon, "watch now and come to believe that through him all things are possible."

Suddenly, to the great astonishment of the crowd, the staff turned into a large snake, fell onto the platform and began to crawl toward the base of a statue of the lion-headed goddess. The crowd was now totally under the control of the priest and his deacon. Some fell to their knees while others sobbed uncontrollably and praised the greatness of the priest.

"And now my friends," said the deacon, "if any of you are ill and wish to be cured today, come forward. This great priest will share the healing powers of Sekhmet with you. If there are those that are blind, lead them forward. Bring the deaf forward and their ears will be opened."

There was a surge toward the platform as those who had stopped only to watch out of curiosity were now eager to benefit from the healing hands of the priest. And more importantly, they were equally eager to hear whatever religious lesson he was prepared to share with them.

At the back of the crowd, fascinated by what he was observing, stood Jesus.

This was the fourth day that Jesus had come to the temple to watch how the priest and his deacon completely captivated their audiences before they shared the special truths and precepts of their temple worship with them. Today, however, Jesus had determined to return to the temple after the demonstrations and lessons were completed and talk with the priest and his deacon.

"Good evening, Friends," said Jesus as he casually approached a small door at the back of the temple later that evening. He had seen a light and, approaching slowly, noticed the priest and his deacon seated at a table in a small room.

"Good evening," said the deacon. "Our services for the day have been completed. If you wish something special from the great priest of the temple of Sekhmet, you will need to return tomorrow."

"Oh, I wish nothing special," said Jesus. " I have traveled to Egypt from a small town north of Jerusalem, and I want only to sit for a moment and talk with you."

"Come in, traveler," said the priest. "Please. Have a seat and join us for a slice of cheese and some good Egyptian beer."

Jesus smiled at the two and gladly accepted what they offered.

At first, they spoke of nothing important.

"How was your trip? Were the roads dangerous? Was the weather bad? Do you have friends whom you are visiting?"

Jesus answered all their questions in a friendly manner and asked them about minor aspects of their daily lives. He had such honest eyes and such a friendly demeanor that the priest and the deacon took an immediate liking to him. Before the evening was over, they invited him to stay with them in an extra room in the temple so they could get to know each other better in the days to come.

After Jesus had watched the two men at work for several more days, he finally decided to talk with them about what they were doing with the crowds that visited the temple each day.

"Is the magic necessary?" asked Jesus.

"Absolutely," replied the deacon with a friendly laugh. "We have to get their attention first if we ever want them to sit still for our religious teachings."

"Would you be upset if we talked about the cures you perform?" asked Jesus.

The deacon looked over at the priest.

The priest considered the question of Jesus for a while before replying.

"No. It wouldn't bother me. What would you like to talk about?" asked the priest.

"Well," observed Jesus, "some of the minor cures you offer are obviously brought about simply by the minds of those who believe that you will heal them."

"Yes, that's true," said the priest. "The mind is a very powerful instrument in governing the health of a person."

"I have noticed, however," said Jesus, now proceeding very carefully so as not to antagonize his hosts, "that the more serious and dramatic healings are carefully staged and involve people that you enlist to help you with your work."

"For example?" asked the deacon, proceeding with equal care into an area that was obviously going to be very sensitive.

"For example," said Jesus, "I noticed that the blind man to whom you restored sight, had no trouble walking trough the streets to get to your temple, and only seemed to lose his sight when he reached the temple precinct."

"And?" said the priest, wondering if Jesus was about to turn on the two of them and cause trouble.

"Well," said Jesus, "I know that you have explained how necessary it is to capture the attention of your audience to get them to accept your religious teachings, but I don't know if you realize that it is not necessary to deceive those whom you wish to reach."

"What are you suggesting?" asked the priest. "That we locate people who are actually blind and restore their sight to them?"

"It is possible, you know," said Jesus.

"Do you have some special magic that you would care to share with us?" asked the deacon.

"Oh, I have something special, but it is not magic as you would use the word."

"What do you have?" asked the priest.

"I have two things," said Jesus, "both of which I would be willing to share with you."

"I see," said the priest now beginning to grow suspicious of their guest. "And how much do you intend that we pay you for your secrets?"

"They are not secrets," said Jesus, "and I don't intend to charge you anything for them, just as you have charged me nothing to remain with you all these days and have freely shared your food and drink with me."

"Well then," said the deacon, "let's hear what you have."

"I have a Father in Heaven with whom all things are possible," said Jesus, "and I have absolute faith that he will do for me whatever I ask of him."

"Faith?" asked the priest. "Do you expect to make the blind see simply by having faith?"

"My friend," said Jesus, "consider the seed of a mustard plant. It is very tiny, isn't it?"

"Very," said the deacon.

"Yet that tiny seed never doubts for a moment that it will grow into a huge tree, does it?" asked Jesus.

"Apparently not," said the deacon, smiling at the clever personification.

"Well, let me tell the both of you that if you had the faith of that mustard seed and trusted my Father in Heaven, you could tell any huge tree to uproot itself and throw itself into the Nile River, and it would do it."

"A tree firmly rooted in the ground?" asked the deacon.

"Yes, and furthermore, if you had absolute faith in my Father in Heaven, you could order mountains to move and they would."

"You actually believe this?" asked the priest.

"I do. And I believe that if I asked my Father in Heaven to help me restore vision to a blind person, he would do it. I also have faith that my Father in Heaven would help me restore hearing to the deaf."

"And heal the lame?" asked the priest.

"And cure lepers, and cast out demons and enable the dumb to speak," said Jesus.

"And you really believe that this can be done?" asked the priest.

"With my Father's help," said Jesus.

"Do you realize what a crowd you could draw?" asked the deacon.

"No doubt a considerable one," replied Jesus. "And the time will come when I will need to command the attention of God's people in Judea to get them to hear the message that I have been sent to give them. That is when my faith will lead my Father in Heaven to grant all my prayers."

"Can your powers be shared with others?" asked the priest who was slowly coming to realize that his guest might just have some truly outstanding abilities.

"Anyone who worships my Father in Heaven, the God of Moses whom the Pharaohs once held captive with his people here in Egypt, and has the faith even of a small mustard seed, can work wonders for the people of God," said Jesus.

"And what makes you think that the God of Moses, your Father in Heaven, is more powerful than Sekhmet whose worship we conduct in this temple?" asked the priest.

"Realize," said Jesus, "that I answer in all kindness and with full gratitude for your hospitality when I say that if Sekhmet had the power to let the blind see, you would not need to have special arrangements with those whom you claim to cure each day."

"Your point is well taken, my friend," said the priest.

"I'm glad that you still consider me your friend," said Jesus.

"And can anyone come to believe in your Father in Heaven, or is He only available to those whom Moses led out of Egypt."

"My Father in Heaven will welcome all who love Him and follow His commands."

"That is very generous of Him," said the deacon.

"Indeed it is," said Jesus. "And speaking of generosity, I wish to thank the both of you for yours over these many days. Tomorrow I will take my leave and continue my travels."

"Where will you go next?" asked the deacon.

"First I intend to visit a cave in Assuit where my parents and I stayed when I was very young."

"It will take you at least seven days to walk to Assuit."

"It will be worth the walk," said Jesus. "In fact, there are two different caves there in which we stayed for a while before we returned to Judaea."

"And after that?"

"Then I will return to the port of Jeddah on the border of the Red Sea and seek those who may know of the wise men who were once called the Magi," said Jesus.

"We shall prepare food and drink for you in the morning to take on your travels," said the deacon.

"There is no need for that," said Jesus. "My Father in Heaven shall look out for me as I travel and will provide all that is needed."

"Well, then," said the priest, "may your Father in Heaven protect you and bring you safely home to your own people."

"And may you have peace on your journey," said the deacon.

"And may the peace of my Father in Heaven be also with you," said Jesus as he turned to enter his room and take his night's rest.

He would be on his way in the morning before his hosts awoke.

By midmorning the following day, Jesus was already a good ten miles outside of Alexandria when he was hailed by a young man hurrying to catch up with him.

"Good morning. Wait up, and I'll walk with you," called the young man.

Jesus stopped and turned to welcome his fellow traveler with a warm smile.

"And how are you today?" asked Jesus.

"A little out of breath. You certainly walk fast. I've been trying to catch up with you for the past mile or so," said the young man.

"I guess I do have a good pace," said Jesus. "But I enjoy a brisk walk."

"Well, if you wouldn't mind slowing your pace just a little, I'd like to walk with you. I find that my time on the road goes a lot faster when I have someone to talk to."

As the two travelers settled into a pace that was comfortable, they began to get acquainted. Jesus explained that, after visiting Assuit in the south, he would return north to cross the narrows of the Red Sea and visit Jeddah.

"Oh, that's a lot farther than I'm going," said the young man.

"What is your destination?" asked Jesus.

"Well, actually, I'm only going about another 70 miles to the town of Busiris."

"Do you have family there?"

"No, I'm going to buy a piece of land about two miles outside of town."

"Are you going to farm the land?" asked Jesus.

"No. I'm just going to buy it," said the young man, who then suddenly became very quiet.

Jesus asked no more questions, and the two of them walked along in silence for at least a mile. Finally the young man spoke again.

"You know, Friend, you have an honest face. Can I trust you with some secret information?"

"I shall respect your privacy if you care to share a secret with me," said Jesus, smiling.

The young man then launched into an explanation of his and his family's business dealings.

"My father and I are merchants," began the young man. "We both lived and worked in Alexandria before I sold my home and my shop to make this trip."

"I understand," said Jesus.

"Well, there's more. My father is a very shrewd business man who made a great fortune when he was young, and I am trying to follow in his footsteps."

"And how did your father make his great fortune?"

"Well, he began as a dealer in pearls—there is a great pearl trade in Alexandria, you know. He had a small shop and was earning enough to support himself. But then, one day, he came across an extremely valuable pearl that was being sold by a diver who had just found it that morning. My father knew that if he could obtain that pearl, he could sell it for a small fortune to one of the royal families."

"So, I assume he bought the pearl," said Jesus.

"Yes, but it wasn't easy. The diver knew he had found something very special and was demanding a high price for it. So my father asked him to hold it for him for one day, and assured him that he would be back the next day and pay him what he was asking."

"Did the diver agree?"

"Yes. So my father went back to his shop and sold his entire inventory of pearls to another dealer in order to come up with the coins he needed. And was it ever worth it! Within a few days, he was able to sell the precious pearl for twenty times what he paid for it."

"And that's how he made his great fortune," observed Jesus.

"And that's sort of what I'm trying to do too," said the young man.

"Are you also a pearl merchant?"

"No. But the last time I was doing business in Busiris, I happened to discover a great treasure just outside of town buried in a field where I was digging a fire pit to prepare a little food. It is a huge treasure and one that I could not dig up and remove without being noticed. So I carefully covered it back up and hurried back to Alexandria to discuss my find with my father. It was he who told me that I needed to purchase the field from its owner so I would have all the rights to the treasure before I started to remove it."

"And that's why you sold your home and your shop," observed Jesus.

"Exactly. And since I am carrying a quantity of gold coins with me, I thought it would be wise to travel as much of the distance as possible with someone I could trust. I can trust you, can't I?" asked the young man.

"More than anyone else in the world," said Jesus, matter-of-factly.

As Jesus and his young friend approached the Nile River, which the young man would need to cross to get to Busiris, they stopped to rest for a while and watch local fishermen work their nets.

"Notice what they are doing?" said Jesus.

"Yes. They seem to be throwing some of their catch away," said the young man.

"Why don't you ask them about it?" suggested Jesus.

The young man got up and walked over to one of the men working the nets and stood watching quietly for a while.

"Did you want something?" asked the fisherman.

"My friend and I were watching you, and we were wondering why you were throwing some of your catch away," said the young man.

"In this river," began the fisherman, "you never know what you're going to snag in your nets. There are a lot of good fish in it, but there are also a lot fish that nobody will buy. So we just lower the nets and haul it all in. Then we sort out what we don't want and throw it back in to swim out to sea. It's a lot faster than just trying to catch exactly what we want."

The young man thanked the fisherman and returned to Jesus to share what he had been told.

"That's how it will be at the end of the world," said Jesus after he listened to the explanation given by the fisherman.

"How's that?" asked the young man.

"The angels of our Father in Heaven will come down and separate the wicked from the just."

"You mean the wicked will be thrown into the water to float out to sea?"

"No, they won't get off that easy," said Jesus. "They will be cast into a furnace of fire."

"That sounds harsh."

"It will be harsh," said Jesus. "There will be wailing and gnashing of teeth."

At that, Jesus and the young man made their way across the river and continued their travel. When they finally came in view of Busiris, the young man took his leave.

"Well, my friend," said the young man, "this is where we must part ways. I wish you safe journeys to Assuit and Jeddah."

"And I wish you success with the purchase of your field. May the peace of our Father in Heaven be with you."

"And also with you," said the young man as he waved goodbye. "And let's both try to be just," added the young man as a parting thought. "We don't want to end up in that furnace."

Jesus smiled and waved. Then he turned and continued on his own journey.

Chapter 7

Jesus Visits Mt. Sinai

"Peace!" said a young traveler whom Jesus met while returning from Assuit. "Are you also a tourist?"

"Peace!" replied Jesus. "Why, yes. I guess I am."

"Would you like to travel together?" asked the young man.

"That depends on where you are going," said Jesus.

"Well, I'm on my way to visit Mt. Sinai and see where Moses was given the tablets of the law by God."

"Is it far from here?" asked Jesus.

"It's in a land called Midian, and to get there we'll have to spend many days crossing the desert of this part of Egypt until we get to the crossing that Moses used to pass through the Red Sea."

"I see," said Jesus.

"Of course, since Moses won't be there to separate the waters for us, we shall have to hire a boat to carry us across. I would guess we have a good walk ahead of us. But we can take our time since we're not being chased by an army like Moses and the Israelites were. Are you up for it?"

"I believe I am," answered Jesus.

"I see that you travel light," said the young man. "Don't you carry a bed roll, extra cloaks and food and wine with you?"

"No, I don't."

"How do you provide for yourself?"

"I find that I am usually provided for."

"And what about those things that are not provided?" asked the young man.

"What is not provided, I do without," said Jesus. "You see, I place all my trust in my Father in Heaven."

"Well," said the young man, "this should be a very interesting trip indeed."

Jesus and his new companion traveled together, getting to know each other and trading stories. Late in the third day, they found themselves approaching a settlement of homes gathered around a large estate that obviously belonged to a very wealthy person. Although they were still a considerable distance from the settlement, the air was filled with the aroma of roasting meat.

"Someone must be planning to have a party," suggested the young man.

"Judging from the columns of smoke and the pleasant aromas, I would guess that preparations are being made for a wedding," said Jesus.

No sooner had Jesus made his observation, than they both noticed a column of men on horseback filing out of the estate entrance and riding in all directions along the several roads in the area.

"Looks like we're going to have company," said the young man as he watched a pair of horsemen hastening toward them.

"They appear to be in good humor," observed Jesus, "so I don't think they mean us any harm."

"Hail, Friends," said one of the men as he came within distance. "This is your lucky day. You are both invited to join in the wedding feast of our master at the large estate you see in the distance. He would like you to hurry because his oxen and fatted calves are already roasting and all things are prepared for the celebration."

At that, the two men hurried past them in search of others to invite.

"That sounds like it could be interesting," said the young man. "Should we accept the invitation?"

"Do you have a nice garment that you could wear to a wedding?" asked Jesus.

"Why, yes," said the young man, "I just happen to have a nice garment with me. How about you?"

"I travel only with the clothes on my back," said Jesus. "But don't let that stop you. It sounds like there will be plenty of food."

"What will you do?" asked the young man.

Jesus looked around a bit and finally focused on a nearby house that looked friendly.

"I'll go over to that house and visit for a while. I'm sure they will welcome me and offer me food and a place to sleep. Then, if you like, we'll meet afterwards and continue our journey together."

"Sounds good," said the young man. "Let's go under that tree so I can change my clothes. Then, if you wouldn't mind, would you be able to take care of my pack until tomorrow?"

"Gladly," said Jesus. "Would you like some friendly advice before you go?"

"Of course," said the young man. "Have you had some experience at attending weddings given by the wealthy?"

"A little," said Jesus.

"Well, then. I'm listening."

"When you enter the dining area," began Jesus, " do not recline in any of the places of honor on the couches as they may be reserved for special guests."

"What do you suggest?"

"I would suggest that you take the lowest place on one of the couches and make yourself comfortable there. That way you won't be embarrassed if the host comes over and asks you to give up your place to someone else. And, you never know. He may even take a liking to you and even ask you to move up into a more honorable spot."

"Sounds like good advice," said the young man.

"At the weddings that I've attended," continued Jesus, "I've noticed that whoever tries to set himself up in a place of honor without being invited usually ends up getting embarrassed by being asked to move, while those guests who humbly take lower spots are frequently honored publicly by being asked to move up higher."

"Thanks," said the young man. "Since it looks like the party is going to last late into the night, I probably won't see you again until morning."

"Enjoy yourself," said Jesus. "I'll take care of your belongings for you until then."

The young man made his way to the main gate of the large estate, and Jesus left the road to walk toward the friendly house he had noticed. As he drew near, he could see, judging by the number of servants who were busy working both around and in the house, that it, too, was the home of a fairly prosperous person.

"Good evening," said Jesus when one of the servants working in the yard noticed him approaching.

"Good evening," said the servant. "Are you not going to the wedding at the large estate? Everyone has been invited?"

"I was also invited," said Jesus, "but I travel light and do not have a garment suitable for such a grand occasion. I was wondering if you would mind if I spent the evening with you folks."

"As far as I'm concerned," said the servant, "you're more than welcome, but we'll have to check with the chief steward."

When Jesus was taken to the chief steward, he, too, proved to be a friendly person who was more than happy to extend hospitality to travelers.

"Our master is not at home," said the steward, "but it is his policy to welcome all travelers."

"Thank you," said Jesus.

"There is one thing, however," cautioned the steward, "that may cause you a little inconvenience."

"What's that?" asked Jesus.

"Well, we were in the process of preparing a nice evening meal for our master when he was suddenly invited to attend the wedding celebration at the estate. So we will not be serving that meal until he returns. It is our custom always to wait for him before we eat so that we can serve him first before we dine on the leftovers."

"That will be no great inconvenience," said Jesus. "I had a bite to eat earlier in the day, and I don't think that I will starve to death."

"We would be happy," continued the steward, "if you would go in and sit with us. We'll all have a little something to drink while we await our master's return."

Jesus gladly accepted their invitation. As he sat and drank what was offered to him, he noticed that, even in the master's absence, all of the servants were going about their duties as expected.

The dining couches were carefully prepared, and the food for the evening meal was being kept warm in the kitchen. Lamps were lit, floors were swept, and even the yard around the outside of the house had been picked up and raked smooth. When the farm animals had all been properly cared for, the rest of the servants slowly began to gather and sit with Jesus to talk. When the steward entered, he secured the door of the house behind him and joined the group.

As they all sat talking quietly, Jesus soon realized that none of them intended to retire for the night before their master returned. As the second watch began, a fresh pitcher was brought in so that cups could be refilled, and, occasionally, the cooks would return to the kitchen to be sure that the food was being kept warm.

The night was more than half gone when the whole group suddenly became silent.

"He's coming," said one of them. "I recognize his step."

The steward, however, did not get up to open the door and check.

"Our instructions are," said the steward who noticed the puzzled look on the face of Jesus, "not to open the door unless someone knocks first. Often, people simply pass by in the night. Some are lost and some are just looking around for whatever. Our master says they are to be ignored unless they knock."

"I understand," said Jesus. "Your master is a very wise man."

Just then, as they all sat quietly listening, there was a feint rap at the door.

"Master!" said the steward who immediately jumped up and opened the door.

"You're all still up!" exclaimed the master who had obviously rapped very lightly to see if they had gone to sleep in his absence.

"Of course, Master," said the steward. "And we have your meal ready and waiting for you as usual. Please come and recline and we shall serve you."

"Not tonight," said the master in a very cheerful tone. "The wedding was wonderful, and I feel so good that tonight I want all of you to take your places on the dining couches, and I will serve you this time."

"Master, we are honored," said the steward. "And, Master, we have a guest whom we welcomed as you would have wanted us to. His name is Jesus, and he has traveled from Nazareth in Judea."

"Our guest is also welcome. Please have him recline in the place of honor as is fitting for one who has traveled so far."

Jesus was amazed at the kindness and humble generosity of the master and graciously accepted his invitation to join them for a much belated evening meal. He almost couldn't believe it, however, when the master began to remove the sandals of each person reclining and to wash their feet.

"This is truly a very humble man," thought Jesus to himself.

The next day, the traveling companion of Jesus came to the house as arranged, and they both took their leave of the generous master and his faithful servants.

"How was the wedding?" asked Jesus after they were back on the road.

"You were right," said the young man. "There was more than enough to eat. There was, however, a rather frightening situation that came up almost immediately after everyone had reclined for the feast."

"What was that?" asked Jesus.

"Well, as might be expected," said the young man, "the master of the estate made a grand entrance and was applauded by all in attendance. At first he seemed pleased to see so many people at the celebration, but then his mood changed abruptly."

"What was the cause?" asked Jesus.

"He happened to spot a guest who was wearing an ordinary work tunic. Not only was it dirty, but it was even ripped in several places."

"What did the master do?"

"Well, after he approached the man in a non-threatening manner, he said, 'Friend, how did you come to this wedding without having a proper garment for the celebration?' The man just looked at him and said nothing, and that's when the master lost his temper. He ordered his servants to tie the man's hands and feet, drag him outside and toss him out into the darkness."

"Many are called, but few are chosen," observed Jesus.

"That would seem to be the case," agreed the young man, as they continued on their way toward their Red Sea crossing.

"See that pillar?" asked the young man as he and Jesus finally came in sight of the water.

"Yes," said Jesus. "What does it mark?"

"I'm told that it shows where Moses divided the waters. There should be another one on the other side. They were supposedly set up by King Solomon to mark the spot 500 years after the Exodus."

When the two travelers arrived at the pillar, they saw several boats and ferrymen ready to carry travelers across in their boats for a fee. Since Jesus carried no money, his companion offered to pay their way.

As Jesus and his traveling companion were being ferried across, the ferryman was a wealth of information.

"This is actually the most shallow part of these waters," he said. "It is, in fact, the part through which Moses led the Israelites."

"How can you be sure?" asked the young man.

"Just wait. When we go a little farther, you can look over the side where the water is very clear. I'll show you where you can see some of the chariots of the Pharaoh's army that were swallowed up by the sea. They're still down there. That's all the proof I need."

And sure enough, before too long, the ferryman let the boat coast to a standstill.

"Now," he said, "Look over the sides. See 'em? They're way down there! There's the back end of a chariot with its handrails. And there! Over there! There's a chariot drawbar sticking straight up out of the bottom."

"Look!" said the young man. "There's a chariot wheel just lying on the bottom!"

"That's nothing!" said the ferryman. "Divers even go down when the water is low to bring up rusty swords and spears. You'll be able to buy some when we get to the other side. There are stands everywhere that sell them—of course, most of them are fakes. But if you have a good eye, you can pick out the real ones."

Jesus and his traveling companion decided to spend that night near the opposite shore. The young man never ceased to be amazed at how easily Jesus made friends, and how readily they were always welcomed into the homes of total strangers and offered food and lodging. The young man wasn't complaining. It was just very different from the way he usually traveled.

In the morning, they asked directions and were told that the high mountain on which God spoke to Moses was 30 miles to the east—another two days journey through desert conditions.

When they reached the area near Mt. Sinai, they both stood in awe of its size. They picked a spot to camp and began to look around.

"Would you like a guide?" asked a very small, but energetic young boy who quickly approached their campsite. "I can show you all of the sights. I've lived here all my life, and I know things that no other guides know. I am very cheap. We shall have fun together. Yes?"

"How can we resist such enthusiasm?" asked the young man. "Shall we hire him?"

"Have you eaten today?" Jesus asked the young boy.

"No, sir. I haven't. My father says I should work first and eat later."

"Come," said Jesus. "Sit and eat with us. It is very hot right now. When it gets a little cooler, you can begin to show us around."

The boy was touched by the kind concern of this traveler and eagerly accepted his invitation. Although Jesus' traveling companion was eager to start looking around, he quickly understood how much this kindness meant to their very small guide and sat to rest and chat casually with Jesus and the boy.

"Where shall we begin?" asked the traveler when the day had cooled a little.

"There!" said the young boy. "First I'll take you to see that large rock."

"The one that is split?" asked the young man.

"Yes," said the boy. "That is the rock from which Moses was able to make the water flow. When we get close, you will see how the rock has been worn away by the water that flowed from it."

"Does the water still flow?" asked the young man.

"No. It has not flowed for many, many years. My father says it stopped flowing when the Israelites left the area."

As the three approached the mountain, they could see that the entire top of Mt. Sinai was blackened as if burned by fire. On its eastern side, they saw a large open area. It was indeed an area large enough for all of the Israelites to have stayed and grazed their cattle.

"What are those stones set up at the base of the mountain?" asked the young man.

"My father says that those are the boundary stones that Moses ordered to be set up so the people would not approach too close to the mountain," said the young guide. "Come, I'll show you some altars that were set up by the Israelites."

"Are they the ones that were used to worship pagan gods?" asked the young man.

"Absolutely," said the young boy. "Not everyone knows where to look, but I can even show you where there is a picture that the people of Moses made on a rock. My father says it is a picture of the golden calf the Israelites were worshipping when Moses came down from the mountain."

Jesus and his traveling companion spent several days exploring the area with their young guide, always making sure that he was well fed and rested before beginning each day's tour.

One day as their very small guide sat with them before beginning the day's sightseeing, the boy looked up at Jesus with admiration.

"May I ask how tall you are, Sir?"

"Oh, I would say about four cubits tall," said Jesus.

"I hope that someday I will grow up to be big and tall. My father says I am too little."

"First of all," said Jesus, "there's nothing wrong with being little."

"Why not?" asked the tiny guide.

"Because it's not a permanent condition."

"You mean there is hope for me?"

"Have you ever seen a mustard seed," said Jesus.

"Mustard seeds are very tiny," said the boy.

"You're right. In fact, some say it is the smallest of all seeds. Yet it does not despair for it knows that when it grows up, it will grow to be as big as a tree. So big, in fact, that many birds will come and rest on its branches."

"So do you think if I have the faith of a mustard seed, I will grow up to be as big as you someday?" asked the boy with hope in his eyes.

"Of course," said Jesus. "But, here. First you must have some more to eat. Growing boys must be well fed."

In this way, Jesus and his traveling companion encouraged and looked out for their young guide. And in the end, the young man gave the boy a generous supply of coins so he would not get in trouble with his father.

"And where will you go from here?" asked Jesus as he and his traveling companion sat by their fire on their final night together."

"I intend to travel north," said the young man. "I want to visit Mt. Hor where God told Moses and Aaron to talk to a rock to make it produce water."

"But, of course," said Jesus, "Moses disobeyed the order and struck the rock twice. And for that reason both he and Aaron were not allowed to enter the Promised Land."

"They say that a person can still see the two holes that were struck in the rock by Moses and from which the water flowed."

"And then whereto?" asked Jesus.

"Well, at that point I should be about 80 miles away from Hebron. I think I'll probably travel up into Judea and maybe visit the great Temple in Jerusalem. It's supposed to be one of the most beautiful structures in the world."

"And they are right," said Jesus.

"You've seen it?"

"Many times," said Jesus. "My home is in Nazareth, and we traveled every year to Jerusalem to visit the Temple. I think you will enjoy it."

When they parted in the morning, Jesus continued his journey to the northwest to get around the Gulf of Aqaba before traveling south along the eastern shore of the coast toward the port of Jeddah.

Chapter 8

Jesus Visits the Temple Built by Abraham

It had taken Jesus nearly a month, but he finally reached his destination. On this evening he was staying with an elderly and wise astrologer whom he had met upon arriving at the Red Sea port of Jeddah.

"So," said Jesus as the two sat before a small fire late in the evening, "you actually knew one of the Magi who traveled to Judea twenty years ago to visit a king who was about to be born?"

"Yes, I did. In those days I was living in Midian."

"And where is that?" asked Jesus.

"Midian is near the Gulf of Aqada. It is the land into which the famous leader of the Israelites known as Moses led his people as they escaped the chariots of the Pharaohs."

"Ah, yes," said Jesus. "When the waters parted before him."

"Precisely," said the elderly astrologer. "The wise man I knew was called Melchior. He and several other Magi who lived in the area had studied the teachings of Zoroaster in Persia as young men. There in Arabia they spent their days explaining those teachings to any who wished to learn and spent their evenings studying the stars and constellations. When Melchior had begun to see signs indicating the impending birth of a child destined to become the new king of the tribe of Israel, he consulted another of his Magi friends."

"And what did his friend think of his interpretations of the stars?" asked Jesus.

"Well, his friend, named Balthasar, said that he had also noticed such an indication in his observations. Balthasar, however, said that, as he read it, the baby soon to be born was destined to rule the entire land of Judea and not necessarily just one tribe."

"What prompted them to begin their journey north?"

"At first, Melchior was content simply to have his reading of the birth of a new king confirmed, and he had no intention of traveling to find him," said the elderly astrologer.

"What made him change his mind?" asked Jesus.

"Well, Balthasar suggested that they consult a third student of the teachings of Zoroaster named Gaspar. Melchior said that it was Gaspar who insisted that the three of them travel to Judea so they could be there to pay homage to this new king as soon as possible after his birth. This, he insisted, would validate their study of astrology and all they had learned of the teachings of Zoroaster."

"Did their study of the stars tell them exactly where to look in Judea?" asked Jesus.

"That was a problem, but Gaspar suggested that they simply travel to a capitol city in the area and ask local authorities where to look. He felt certain that they, too, would be aware of such a well-omened event."

"So, I guess that settled it. Did they begin their journey immediately?" asked Jesus.

"Well," said the elderly astrologer, "Gaspar wanted the three of them to set out immediately, but Melchior and Balthasar convinced him that they needed time to prepare. They would have to choose the perfect gifts to be given to such a new born king."

"Yes," said Jesus, "I have heard of the special gifts they took with them."

"Oh, you have? And what were they?" asked the elderly astrologer, looking doubtfully at his guest.

"Gold, frankincense and myrrh."

"And how is it that you know of these gifts?" asked the elderly astrologer.

"You see, my friend," confided Jesus, feeling sure he could trust his host, "I was the child whom the three Magi visited. I am the one who was born to become the new King of the Israelites."

"And why are you not leading your people at this time?"

"The time has not yet come for me to accept my role. But I will tell you more of that later. Please continue with your story," insisted Jesus.

"Well then, Melchior and his two Magi friends finally did set out after a year or so."

"Did you ever see those three Magi again?" asked Jesus.

"Oh, yes. I saw them on their return. And did they have some exciting adventures to relate. They couldn't believe it, but they said the child-king was actually living in a simple house when they visited him. His father was only a poor carpenter and they were pleased to receive their valuable gifts that they said would be used to help care for the child."

"Yes, that's true," said Jesus. "My stepfather has told me how we lived in a small house after I had been born in a cave since that was the only place they could use when we first got to Bethlehem. Many times my mother told me of the visit of the Magi two years after I had been presented in the Temple at Jerusalem."

"Your stepfather?" asked the elderly astrologer.

"Yes, Joseph is my stepfather."

"Who then is your father?"

"My Father is in Heaven," said Jesus very matter-of-factly. "I am the son of the God of Abraham. I am Immanuel, and I was born to serve as the Messiah for the people of God, to be their Savior."

At this, the elderly astrologer became silent. He spent the next half hour alternately staring at Jesus and poking at their small fire with a stick as he let the information shared by his guest sink in.

"And does your Father in Heaven," asked the elderly astrologer, finally breaking his silence, "want you to be a Savior to the Israelites only?"

"No, my friend," said Jesus with a smile. "My Father in Heaven loves all those whom he has created and is willing for all who believe in me to be saved."

"Then there is hope for the rest of us too?" asked the elderly astrologer, now returning the smile of his guest.

"Absolutely!"

The next morning as Jesus was preparing to leave the home of his friend, the elderly astrologer offered a suggestion.

"My friend," he began, "before you leave this region, you may be interested in visiting a small town named Bakkah."

"And what shall I see there?" asked Jesus.

"There," continued the elderly astrologer, "you will be able to visit the shrine that your forefather, Abraham, built to your Father in Heaven. They say he was given construction directions by the angel Gabriel himself."

"And what is the name of this shrine?"

"It is called the Ka'ba."

"And how does one get to Bakkah?" asked Jesus.

"Oh, it's not hard. Bakkah is a small town about 45 miles inland from here. A two or three day walk at most for a young man like you. I will gladly show you the road on which to start your journey. The shrine is small, but one that I believe you will enjoy seeing as it was built in honor of your Father in Heaven."

"My friend," said Jesus, "thank you for all your kind hospitality and for sharing your wisdom and stories with me. And, yes, I believe I will enjoy visiting the Ka'ba."

At that, Jesus and his host left the small house and began walking toward the road that led to Bakkah. After Jesus took leave of his friend, he turned and gave him one more parting smile.

"May the peace of our Father in Heaven be with you," said Jesus.

"And also with you, my friend," said the elderly astrologer before turning to go home.

As Jesus walked away, he thought to himself, "That man has the most pure heart of any I have ever met. He is definitely blessed and will surely see God my Father some day!"

When Jesus arrived at Bakkah two days later, he had little trouble locating the shrine called the Ka'ba. It was, in fact, the focal point of all of the activities of the city. The shrine had become very commercialized, and was surrounded by vendors selling everything from small chips of the magic stone that was placed in the sanctuary of the shrine, to models of the first shrine that had supposedly been built on the site by Adam himself.

"You see," explained a vendor with whom Jesus had struck up a conversation "after Adam and Eve were sent out of Paradise, Adam lived on a mountain on the island of Serendip while Eve lived here in Arabia near the port of Jeddah. Do you know the town?"

"Yes," said Jesus, " I have just traveled from Jeddah."

"Well," continued the vendor, "after being separated from each other for nearly 200 years, their God permitted them to meet again here in this narrow valley."

"Here in Bakkah?" asked Jesus.

"Yes. You see, that's what Bakkah means. A narrow valley."

"I see," said Jesus.

"And Adam was so happy to see Eve again that he asked his God if a shrine could be built here just like the one at which they had worshipped their God in Paradise. And, of course, God granted his wish, and this, my friend, is a model of the shrine that was built."

"And where, exactly, was Adam's shrine located?" asked Jesus.

"Why, on the very spot now occupied by the Ka'ba. You see, Abraham was instructed by an angel to build his shrine to the one and only God on the very spot once occupied by the shrine of Adam. How many models would you like to purchase?" asked the vendor.

"None at this time," said Jesus. "But I must say, you certainly have some interesting tales to tell. Very interesting indeed."

Jesus took time to visit the Ka'ba, and looked carefully at the black stone that stood in the sanctuary.

"It was once white," volunteered a young man who happened to be standing near Jesus.

"What was?" asked Jesus.

"The magic sanctuary stone. It is a great white sapphire brought here from the Garden of Eden by the angel Gabriel."

"And how is it that it is now black?" asked Jesus, playing along.

"Do you see that man kneeling to kiss the stone?" asked the young man.

"Yes."

"Well, they say that when worshippers kiss the stone, their sins pass from their lips into the stone. Over the years all those sins have turned the stone black."

Jesus would never cease to be amazed at the stories he heard during his ten years of traveling. Most were told with absolute sincerity even though many seemed to contain very little truth.

"And is this what you believe?" asked Jesus.

"Me? I'm just a tourist. I like to gather local lore and share it with anyone who's interested. And what about you, my friend?" asked the young man. "Are you on a journey?"

"I will next be traveling north into Persia," said Jesus.

"And what is there that you wish to see?"

"It's more whom than what," said Jesus.

"Well, then, for whom will you be looking in Persia?"

"For descendents of the ten lost tribes of Israel," said Jesus.

"Are you related to them?"

"I am a descendent of the House of David. My ancestors belonged to the two tribes of Israel that lived in the south."

"And, of course, there were twelve tribes of Israel," observed the young man.

"Yes. They were descended from the twelve sons of Jacob. Originally, each tribe had settled in a different region on either side of the Jordan River."

"Do you know how the ten tribes got lost?"

"Well," began Jesus, "I have heard that in the ninth year of Hoshea, the king of Assyria invaded Samaria and captured all the members of the northern ten tribes."

"What did he do with them?"

"Some he supposedly took to a place called Halah, and others he resettled on a river of Gozan called the Habor. Still others he put in different cities of Medes."

"And you intend to go in search of their descendents?" asked the young man.

"I intend to travel northeast toward Babylon. After I cross the Tigris and Euphrates Rivers, I shall enter Persia and begin my quest," said Jesus.

"You do realize that you have nearly a thousand mile trip ahead of you, don't you?"

"Yes, I do. I have the time, and it is a journey that I believe I must make," said Jesus.

"Well, my friend," said the young man, "I have no doubt that you will succeed. I'm sure you will make friends wherever you go. I wish you all the best."

"May the peace of God be with you in your travels," said Jesus.

"And also with you," replied the young man.

Chapter 9

Jesus Travels in Persia

Jesus would spend the next two years of his life traveling to the east, meeting people, making friends, learning about local customs, asking questions. He sought descendents of the tribes of Reuven, Shimon, Levi, Yehuda, Issachar, Zevulun, Dan, Naphtali, Gad and Asher with varying degrees of success. Occasionally, he was able to identify some familiar traits, but the customs, beliefs and languages of the people he met little resembled descendents of the two tribes of Abraham with which he was familiar.

Jesus was told that descendents of the tribes of Dan, Aevulun, Asher and Naphtali lived in the mountains in Persia, but this could not be confirmed. Those who shared this information said that the fierceness and self-dependence of these mountain dwellers indicated a relationship with the tribes of Israel.

One old man whom Jesus met told him of a large Jewish settlement near a place called Kheibar.

"But if they indeed are Jews," said the old man, "they have, no doubt, abandoned all the practices passed on to them by Abraham and no longer have any desire to please their God."

"And why do you say that?" asked Jesus

"They are a people prone to looting and violence. From what I have heard of them, I don't think there is any way that they could return to their God even if He did forgive them."

"And where is Keibar?" asked Jesus.

When the old man told Jesus where the supposed Jewish settlement was located and how long it would take to get to the area, Jesus decided to bypass the settlement at this time. Still, he did not share the old man's views. If these violent looters were descendents of Abraham, they were, nevertheless, not beyond hope of salvation.

"You know," said Jesus, "just because a descendent of Abraham leads a wicked life, it does not mean than he must despair of being forgiven by his God."

"I don't know," said the old man. "I've heard they are pretty bad people."

"Let me tell you a little story," said Jesus.

"Alright," said the old man. "I certainly have the time."

"There was once a rich man," began Jesus, "who had loaned money to two of his friends. To one he loaned 500 silver coins, and to the other fifty. After both of his friends fell on bad times, he soon realized that neither would ever be able to pay him back."

"What did he do?" asked the old man. "Have them thrown into prison?"

"No," said Jesus. "They were his friends. He had compassion for them and forgave both of their debts."

"That would be very unusual for a rich man to do in this land," said the old man.

"Perhaps," said Jesus. "But tell me, which of his friends do you suppose was the most grateful for having had his debt forgiven?"

"Without a doubt it would have been the one who no longer had to pay back the 500 silver coins."

"I would agree," said Jesus.

"And who do you suppose would be more grateful to his God if he were forgiven, a man who has repented of a life of violent looting or one who has repented only of a minor theft?"

"No doubt the man who was forgiven for his life of violent looting."

"The God of Abraham loves all of his people, no matter how far they have strayed from the laws of their forefathers. He knows that those to whom more has been forgiven will love Him more. No, my elderly friend," said Jesus, "I would not say that any of God's children are beyond salvation."

Jesus took his leave of his elderly companion, and continued on his journey through Persia. He intended to spend a couple of years in the region and hoped to learn more about the people who lived there and the lives they led. A week or so later, he came into a lush valley, the hills of which were planted in vineyards. It was the fall of the year, and the aroma of ripe grapes filled the air. After taking time to appreciate the beauty of the view, he began to make his way to one of the larger complexes of buildings.

As Jesus drew near, he could see that preparations were well under way for the harvest.

"Master," called one of the servants who had come out of a dirt-covered hut in which large wineskins were stored. "Master there is a large number of empty wineskins that we used last year. Shall we wash them out so they can be used again with the new wine?"

"Absolutely not," replied the master harshly. "If there is old wine left in some of the larger containers, it can be put into the old skins. Don't you know that if you put new wine in an old wineskin, it will burst as the wine works?"

The servant, not wanting to get into any more trouble, immediately disappeared back into the dirt-covered hut.

"Where's the steward?" called the master in a loud voice. "I shouldn't have to be bothered with stupid questions from inexperienced servants."

"Greetings," said Jesus when he had a chance to catch the attention of the master.

"We're not hiring yet," said the master assuming that Jesus was looking for work.

"Oh, I'm not asking to be hired," said Jesus. "I am a traveler in your country, and I was just wondering if I might find a cup of water and a cool place to rest."

The master turned his full attention on his tall, handsome visitor and was immediately taken with his kind appearance and the soothing quality of his voice.

"Of course. Forgive me. You are more than welcome," said the master. "Come with me, and we'll sit together. The rest will do me good."

"Are you not having a good day?" asked Jesus.

"More like a bad week," replied the master.

"It must be very challenging to run a large vineyard such as yours," said Jesus.

"Oh, it wouldn't be so bad if we could hire people with some experience. For instance, two days ago I sent a crew of new men up onto that hill over there to build a small storage hut where we could keep tools and harvest baskets so they wouldn't have to be carried back and forth each day."

"Did they not build it?" asked Jesus.

"Oh, they got it built alright. But the fools built it on a sandy part of the hill. When it rained during the night, the whole thing ended up in a heap at the bottom of the hill and took out a bunch of vines in the process."

"I guess they didn't realize that a foundation has to be built on rock if you want a building to withstand the wind and the rain."

"That's what I mean. They just don't know. And not only do I have to put up with inexperienced servants, but my own sons are giving me grief."

"And how is that?" asked Jesus.

"Oh, I guess they're just being arrogant. They're at that age, you know."

"Would you like to talk about it?" asked Jesus in an attempt to encourage his host to relax a little.

"Well, take this morning, for instance," began the master. "I asked my older son to go into the vineyard and work with the servants to prepare for the harvest."

"Did he agree?"

"No! He refused. He said he had more important things to do. So I went to look for my younger son."

"Did you have better luck with him?" asked Jesus.

"I thought I did. When I asked him to oversee the work in the vineyard, he agreed immediately."

"Well at least he respected your wishes," said Jesus.

"But that's just it," said the master. "He said he would go, but he never went. A total disappointment."

"So were the servants working the vineyard left unsupervised?" asked Jesus.

"Well, not really. Turned out my older son had a change of heart later in the morning and went out and took care of the work."

"Well, that was good," said Jesus. "Is your vineyard large?"

"One of the largest in the valley. In fact, tomorrow I need to go into that small town you can see in the distance and try to hire additional people to help with the harvest. Do you have a place to stay tonight?" asked the master.

"I stay where I am welcome," replied Jesus.

"Well, you are certainly welcome here," said the master. "I'll have my steward show you where you can sleep and get something to eat. You'll be my guest."

The next morning, Jesus was up early, but the master had already left for town to hire his workers. While he was gone, Jesus had a chance to spend a little time talking with the master's older son.

"Your father was telling me how much he relies on you and your younger brother to help run the vineyard," began Jesus, not wanting to indicate that he heard that the two boys were somewhat less than reliable.

"My younger brother?" shot back the son. "I tell you, things were a lot better around here before he came back. I respect my father, but my heart hasn't really been in my work here ever since my brother's little fling."

"I'm sorry," said Jesus, "I didn't mean to open a sore subject."

"Well, if you're going to be around here very long, you might as well hear about it. Someone's bound to bring it up sooner or later."

Jesus sat and gave the older boy his full attention. He realized that the boy had a lot on his mind and wanted a chance to talk about it.

"You see, about six months ago my younger brother decided to leave. He saw no future for himself here on the vineyard. He figured that I would probably inherit most of the place anyway after our father passed away since I'm the oldest."

"So he just left?" asked Jesus.

"Not before he talked my father into giving him his fair share of our inheritance. Well, Father had to sell a section of our vineyard to a neighbor to come up with a ready supply of silver coins, but he finally handed over what he figured my brother had coming."

"Where did your brother go?" asked Jesus.

"Oh, he wanted to get as far away from here as possible. He said some pretty harsh things about how backwards he thought we all were and how we would never be any better than a bunch of farmers all our lives and how he wanted no part of it any more. He was going to go somewhere and make something great out of himself."

"I guess things didn't work out as he thought they would," observed Jesus.

"That's just the problem as far as I'm concerned," said the older son. "Once he wasted his inheritance on fancy living in the big city, he had no choice but to go back to the only thing he knew."

"Farming?" asked Jesus.

"Except that the only way he could get work was to hire on as a feeder on a pig farm. And the pay was so bad that he could barely afford to feed himself. Then I guess he just sort of wised up one day and realized how nice he used to have it back here with us."

"So he came back," said Jesus.

"Yeah, and I guess that wouldn't have been so bad in itself—we could certainly use his help—if only my father hadn't made such a big thing about it."

"Don't you imagine that your father was glad to have your brother back?" asked Jesus.

"Oh, sure he was. But you should have seen him. Made a complete fool out of himself as far as I'm concerned," said the older son.

"What did he do?" asked Jesus.

"I happened to be working with some men on the other side of that hill over there, so I didn't see it, but I heard about it afterwards. As soon as he saw my brother trudging up the road, he took off running to meet him. I guess he just sort of lost it and started hugging and kissing him and feeling all sorry for him because he looked skinny and his tunic was filthy and ragged."

"How did you learn that your brother had returned?" asked Jesus.

"Well, as the men and I were coming home at the end of the day, we could smell meat roasting. Then, as we got closer, we heard music and saw the makings of quite a celebration—all for a kid who thought he was too good to live and work with the rest of us. What really got to me, however, was when I saw my brother all decked out in one of my father's best robes. He was even wearing nice shoes and had one of my father's gold rings on his finger, a ring I had always hoped to have some day."

"Well," said Jesus, trying to calm the older brother down a little, "you really can't blame your father for being glad to have your brother back. He was probably worried about him."

"I suppose so," said the older son, "but he didn't have to go overboard like that. Why, just a month earlier I had asked him if we couldn't kill the fatted calf so I could have a little party to thank the men that were working especially hard to make up for the help we lost when my younger brother left."

"What did your father say?" asked Jesus.

"He refused, of course. He said there was a time to celebrate and a time to work and that it just wasn't the time to celebrate. He still wasn't over the fact that his youngest son had abandoned him, I guess."

"So, how did you and your father resolve everything?" asked Jesus. "He obviously picked up on the fact that you were upset with the party."

"Well, when I had a chance to talk to him the next day, I reminded him how hard I had been working with him all these years. I pointed out that I could always be relied on to do everything he asked. I reminded him that he had refused to let me have a party, but then turned right around and roasted the fatted calf for my brother who wasted all his inheritance on wine and loose women so far as we knew."

"So what did your father say to that?" asked Jesus.

"He could see how hurt I was, but all he could do was remind me that, someday, as the eldest son I would still be inheriting everything that was his. He said I shouldn't begrudge him if he wanted to celebrate because the son that he thought was dead was alive. He just kept repeating, 'I thought your brother was lost, and now I have found him again.' I finally felt sorry for him and decided to let the whole thing drop. But I have to admit that my heart just isn't in the work anymore. Not with my younger brother around."

"Your father did mention that you initially refused to do what he asked of you yesterday," said Jesus.

"So he shared that little incident with you, did he?" asked the older son. "I hope he also told you what a little liar my brother is. 'Oh, sure, Father. No problem. I'll get right out there and take care of that.' And then he goes off and does his own thing, knowing, of course, that I would come around and not let Father down."

"You did the right thing," said Jesus. "Hopefully, your good example will encourage your younger brother to act responsibly and respect your father's wishes."

"He'd better if he wants to stay around here much longer. If not, if anything ever happens to our father, I'll send the kid packing before he knows what hit him," threatened the older son. "As far as I'm concerned, he's no better than a sack of salt that has gone bad. The only thing you can do with it is to throw it out. Can't even use it for fertilizer!"

In a while, Jesus and the older son saw the master returning with the men he had hired. The oldest son excused himself and went off to do his day's work.

As it turned out, even though the master was able to hire a number of good men, by midday he decided that more were needed and quickly returned to town to hire whomever else he could find.

"You know," said the master who came over a couple hours later to talk to Jesus when he saw him watching the work. "I'll bet if I went back into town right now and hired just a few more men, we could have that whole section of vines picked clean by nightfall."

"I think you're right," said Jesus. "You have a good group working up there, and it wouldn't take many more men to finish it."

And, as they hoped, by nightfall all the grapes had been harvested from that section of the vineyard. The workers came down off the hills and began to gather to receive their pay.

"Well done," said the master. "Now if you will all line up, the steward will give you each the silver coin we agreed on."

"Hold on," spoke up one of the workers who had been hired early that morning. "You mean that these guys who came at midday and later in the afternoon are going to get the same pay as those of us who worked and sweated all day?"

"It's what you all agreed to," said the master.

"But we didn't know we could have earned just as much by only working a few hours. It's not fair!"

"He's right," shouted the others who had also been hired early in the morning. "It's not fair!"

"Listen, Friend," shouted the master, addressing the man who had spoken up first. "I'm not going back on my word. Didn't you agree to work for me for one silver coin? Take what you've earned and go. I'll give each man what I promised. It's not against the law for me to do what I want with my own money."

As it was now getting dark and the workers had a long walk back to town, they finally decided to accept the pay that was promised and leave. When the last had gone, Jesus tried to comfort his host once again since the man was definitely showing the strains of a long, hard day.

"It seems to me that you treated all those men fairly," said Jesus. "You shouldn't trouble yourself with their grumbling."

"Why do people always have to give the old evil eye to someone who chooses to be a little generous? It's not their money he's giving away. I just know I'm going to have a lot of trouble in town from now on just because I try to do the right thing."

"Well," said Jesus, "I personally think that those people who are persecuted for doing the right thing are blessed in my Father's eyes and that the Kingdom of Heaven will be theirs some day."

"Maybe so, but in the meantime I'm going to get a lot of grief," said the master.

"My friend," comforted Jesus, "someday they will learn that you have acted exactly as my Father in Heaven. Just as you have done with those whom you hired, my Father often allows those who try to be first to be last, while those that end up being last he often allows to be first."

"That's how it usually works out," said the master. "Come. Tonight I would be honored to have you dine with me."

The next day, as Jesus prepared to leave, he had an opportunity to spend a little time with the steward of the estate who had been instructed to see that Jesus was properly fed before he continued his journey.

"It is a shame that the two brothers don't get along," said Jesus.

"Oh," said the steward, "I wouldn't worry about them. They're better than they used to be. I talk to them individually whenever I have a chance. I think that before too long I'll have them enjoying the same warm relationship they once enjoyed as children. Their father is a good man and certainly deserves to see them happy."

"Then you are a true child of God yourself," said Jesus.

"And why is that?" asked the steward.

"Because you have adopted the role of peacemaker. And now, my friend," continued Jesus," may the peace of my Father in Heaven be with you."

"And also with you," returned the steward. "And may He keep you safe in your travels."

Chapter 10

Jesus Crosses the Indus River
And Befriends a Buddhist Priest

During the two years that Jesus traveled in Persia, he became impressed with the wisdom of occasional scholars he happened to meet. Many were men who were absolutely dedicated to the pursuit of truth, and who sincerely endeavored to lead lives of merit.

The further east Jesus traveled, the more he began to hear of a group of holy men who were known as Buddhists. These men, he was told, had developed a very moral philosophy and taught their followers to lead an ethical way of life. These Buddhists also stressed the importance of growing in maturity and perfection until a sort of love of all people and things was attained.

"If these people," thought Jesus to himself, "do not believe in my Father in Heaven, they at least seem to be striving to live lives that would be pleasing to him."

Jesus continued to travel east until he came to the Indus River. It was after he crossed the river that he was finally able to meet, in person, a holy man who was introduced to him as a Buddhist priest.

"And who was this Buddha that you revere?" asked Jesus after becoming friendly with his new acquaintance.

"Oh, his name was not really Buddha," said the priest in a jovial, sing-song tone.

"What was his name?"

"His name was Siddharta Gautama. His father was called Suddhodana, a powerful man who ruled a district near the Himalayan Mountains."

"And why is he called Buddha?" asked Jesus.

"I can see," said the priest, "that you are truly interested. If you are willing to spend time with me, I will gladly teach you the basics of our beliefs."

"Are they complicated?" asked Jesus.

"Not really. But there are several areas to cover. And once they are covered, you will find that it may take years to understand

95

completely what you have been taught and even longer if you wish to practice our beliefs in your daily life."

"I have the time," answered Jesus, "if you have the patience."

"Oh, no problem," said the priest in his friendly tone of voice.

"So," said Jesus, "why is Gautama called Buddha?"

"Well, when Gautama was a young boy, he lived in a palace and was kept very protected from the realities of life around him. His father did not want him to experience any of life's unpleasantness. One day, however, Gautama took a trip outside the palace walls. He was almost immediately confronted by four sights that changed the way he thought of life."

"What four things did he see?" asked Jesus.

"He saw an old man, a sick man, a dead man and a beggar."

"None of whom he had ever seen before?"

"That's right. The pain and suffering of these four men so troubled Gautama that he immediately left his father's palace and began to travel around trying to find some answers."

"So he, too, undertook a long journey," observed Jesus to himself.

"First he studied the ancient writings preserved by the Saindava people who worshipped an all-powerful god called Brahma, but he soon rejected what they had to teach. He next decided to begin leading a life of complete self-denial in the hope that this would give him the peace he needed in the presence of so much pain and suffering in the world."

"Did it work?" asked Jesus.

"No. All it did was weaken him tremendously. So he then turned to a life of quiet meditation."

"And did his life of quiet meditation have something to do with him being called Buddha?" asked Jesus.

"I see you are very quick, indeed," said the priest. "It absolutely does. One day, while sitting under a fig tree which was his favorite place to meditate, Gautama suddenly found the answers to the problem of pain and suffering with which he had been struggling."

"So the tree was sort of a key to his understanding," said Jesus as he considered the similarity to the Tree of Knowledge in the Garden of Eden.

"Yes," said the priest. "He called the fig tree his Bohdi tree. In our language, bohdi or bohdati means awakening or understanding."

"And what was the understanding that Gautama discovered?" asked Jesus.

"Now that," said the priest with a friendly smile, "is what we shall spend the rest of our time together discussing."

Over the next several months, the priest patiently explained to Jesus the Four Noble Truths that were realized by Gautama and the Eight-fold Path that he worked out to lead his followers to what he considered to be the perfect way to live.

"I can totally agree with your First Noble Truth," said Jesus. "All who live inevitably encounter suffering."

"And how do you personally deal with the suffering in your life?" asked the priest.

"As most people, I try not to focus on the minor aches and pains of daily life. We all have muscles that hurt, occasional headaches and upset stomachs. If we are kind to our bodies and rest and eat properly, we can work through those minor discomforts," said Jesus.

"Yes, but what about pains that appear unbearable and spirit-shaking suffering?" asked the priest.

"That is when I pray to my Father in Heaven and ask for His help."

"Do you expect your Father in Heaven to remove your pain?"

"While I believe that He could if He chose to, I usually just ask Him to give me the strength I need to deal with my suffering. He knows what I am going through, and I believe it is His will that I deal with it as best I can with His help," replied Jesus.

"And how do you feel when you see a beggar suffering, or a sick man suffering or a family grieving over the death of a loved one—three of the sorrows that changed Gautama's life?" asked the priest.

"My heart, of course, goes out to all those who suffer," said Jesus. "If any who suffer were to believe in me, with the help of my Father in Heaven I would do what I could to relieve their suffering."

"And how would you relieve the suffering of those whose loved one has died?" asked the priest.

"If it were the will of my Father in Heaven, I believe that I could ask to have even those who appear to be dead to live again," replied Jesus.

"You have great faith in your Father in Heaven," observed the priest. "Perhaps when you have finished learning from me, you will take the time to teach me to have a similar faith."

"I will not deny your wish, for it is possible for all who believe in me to be loved and accepted by my Father in Heaven," said Jesus.

When the priest finally got around to presenting the Second Noble Truth, once again Jesus found himself to be in agreement with the basic principal taught by Gautama.

"Desire for the things of this world can definitely cause great suffering," agreed Jesus. "Plus they distract a person from the real goal of his life."

"Which is?" asked the priest.

"Eternal happiness with the Father in Heaven," replied Jesus. "There is a saying that a person's heart is where his treasure is. If a person devotes his life to fulfilling selfish desires, experiencing physical pleasures and amassing great wealth, his whole heart and attention will be devoted to these things and he will not be focusing on his eternal happiness in Heaven."

"So then you agree with Gautama that a craving for wealth is a great cause of suffering," said the priest.

"Absolutely. In fact, I would say that it is easier for a camel to pass through the eye of a needle than it is for a rich man to enter the Kingdom of my Father in Heaven," observed Jesus.

"In that case," said the priest, "I believe that you would be ready to accept the Third Noble Truth of Gautama."

"And what is the Third Noble Truth?"

"The Third Noble Truth is that a person can put an end to all of his suffering by ridding himself of all desires."

Jesus considered the statement for a long while in silence.

"Have you nothing to say?" asked the priest. "Does not the Third Noble Truth flow from the Second?"

"Yes and no," said Jesus.

"How so?"

"Well, while it is true that total dedication to satisfying our desires can result in suffering, I believe that man has been created in the image and likeness of his Father in Heaven and that certain desires have been given him for his self-preservation. When our body is hungry, it reminds us that we need to care for it by giving us a desire for food. When it is weary, it reminds us to provide it with rest by giving us a desire for relaxation and sleep. These are all good desires that were given us by the Father in Heaven to remind us to care for our bodies."

"So you believe that some pleasures are good and do not necessarily result in suffering?" asked the priest.

"Yes, I do," said Jesus. "Our Father in Heaven gave us the gifts of this world to enjoy. They are not evil in and of themselves. We encounter suffering and evil when we overindulge our desires. When we live to eat instead of eating to live."

"Well," said the priest after giving some consideration to what Jesus was saying, "what you say does seem to make sense, but I'm afraid that these beliefs of yours in your Father in Heaven and in the basic goodness of certain desires may prevent you from accepting the Fourth Noble Truth and all the rest of the teachings of Gautama."

"Did Gautama not believe in the Creator of the heavens and the earth and of men and all things on the earth?" asked Jesus.

"Gautama believed that there is a condition that is unlike anything we can conceive of in this life. He taught that in that condition—which you may be calling Heaven—none of the things that we have around us on earth exist: no water, air, light, space, nor time. He taught that in that condition there is no arising or passing away, no death, no change, no standing still. In other words, it is impossible for us to imagine or understand that condition, and yet, Gautama taught that our true happiness can only be achieved when we arrive at that condition."

"And what did he call that condition?" asked Jesus.

"He called it Nirvana," said the priest. "As a teacher, Gautama said that his only goal was to show people the way to achieve the condition of Nirvana. He wanted to help people have a better life by showing them the way to the truth."

"I am the way, the truth and the life," said Jesus almost to himself.

"What did you say?" asked the priest.

"I said that I am the way, the truth and the life."

"I don't understand what you are saying," said the priest.

"So," said Jesus, changing the subject, "did Gautama teach his followers that there is any person existing in this condition of Nirvana who looked out for them or would reach out and help them attain the condition? Did he not teach that there is an all powerful God whose condition—as he rightly understood—is totally beyond our understanding and yet takes a personal interest in those He has created?"

"No, he did not," said the priest. "He taught only that Nirvana was a condition for which each must strive to rid himself of suffering and attain a perfect existence."

"That is sad that Gautama believed he had no one to help him achieve his perfection. And what are the steps that Gautama taught must be taken to achieve Nirvana?" asked Jesus.

"Well," said the priest, "before we can get into that, I must first explain the Fourth Noble Truth. That, however, will have to wait for another day since, as you have wisely observed, my body is telling me that it needs rest and food. And, yes, I agree with you. In moderation, these are good things."

Over the days and weeks that followed, it was hard to tell who was the more eager student or teacher, Jesus or the Buddhist priest. They respected each other, enjoyed each other's company and patiently shared information in a non-judgmental manner. They both knew that neither could fully accept all that the other had to offer, but that did not dampen their enthusiasm for the process.

"For those who are ready," began the priest finally, "and able to accept the Fourth Noble Truth, Gautama laid out a very detailed path that would lead each person to his own personal Nirvana."

"And what is this final truth?" asked Jesus.

"The Fourth Noble Truth is that it is possible to extinguish all desire by following an eight-fold path."

"Well, you know from the start that I don't believe that all desires must be extinguished," said Jesus. "They only lead to suffering when followed in excess. But we can agree to disagree on that point. Please continue as I am very interested in the details of

Gautama's eight-fold path. I have to believe that the man had some very valid insights and was not all wrong in his teachings."

"The eight-fold path helps people develop correct habits of living," said the priest.

"See," said Jesus, "I can already agree with you entirely on that point. The whole secret to living life as our Father in Heaven intends for us to live and enjoy it, is to have the correct habits. With our Father's daily help we need to get to the point where we do the right things, react in the proper ways, automatically avoiding situations that cause us to get into trouble with our bodies and our minds. Since habits can make or break a person, teaching a person to have good habits is definitely essential to his happiness."

"The first step on the eight-fold path," said the priest, "is one you have almost already taken."

"And what is that?" asked Jesus.

"The first step is to have the Right Views; that is, you must accept the Four Noble Truths."

"With reservations," said Jesus. "What is the Second Step?"

"Step Two is to have the Right Resolve. A person must renounce all thoughts of lust, bitterness, cruelty, hatred, greed and desires in general. A person must also resolve to harm no living creature."

"That, again, is very wise council, with the understanding that some desires are good and meant to be satisfied in moderation," said Jesus. "And I absolutely agree that all of the creatures of our Father in Heaven deserve respect and should not be needlessly harmed."

"Ah," interrupted the priest, "but it goes much, much farther than that."

"In what way?" asked Jesus.

"When Gautama says that we must harm no living creature, he means that even if we are being attacked by another, we should not return harm for harm."

"Yes. I understood that this was implied in his directive," said Jesus.

"So," said the priest still trying to see how completely Jesus had, in fact, thought the directive through, "what would you do if a man struck you on your cheek? Would you not be inclined to strike him back?"

"No, I would not," replied Jesus.

"What would you do?"

"I would offer my other cheek for him to strike also."

"That is an answer that Gautama would have found acceptable," said the priest.

"He must have indeed been a wise man," observed Jesus.

"Okay," said the priest, "I believe you are now ready to hear Step Three."

"I'm ready."

"Step Three is Right Speech. A person must not lie, slander others or waste time in idle gossip. A person must speak only the truth."

"I am the way, the truth and the life," said Jesus, again more to himself than to his companion.

"What?" asked the priest. Then realizing what it was that Jesus had said, observed, "Oh, you're making that statement again."

"Let those hear who have ears to hear," said Jesus.

"Right," said the priest, choosing to ignore the admonition. "Now, I don't think you will have any objections to Step Four."

"And what is Step Four?" asked Jesus.

"Step Four requires Right Behavior. Gautama taught that to reach Nirvana a person would have to abstain from sexual immorality, stealing, killing, and all anti-social behavior in general."

"Amen," said Jesus. "I can absolutely agree with the teachings of Step Four."

"Amen?" questioned the priest who had not heard the word before.

"It means that I agree. So be it. You're absolutely right."

"Alright then," said the priest. "Amen!"

Jesus and the Buddhist priest spent many pleasant hours discussing the full implications of the first Four Steps, taking time occasionally to go for short walks and enjoy the beauties of each day. During meals they talked of more mundane, non-related matters and during the evenings traded interesting stories about their boyhoods and families and the communities in which they once lived. One evening, as Jesus was relating his experiences in Joseph's workshop, the Buddhist priest used what Jesus was saying to prepare for Step Five that he intended to discuss on the following day.

"So, you were a carpenter?" asked the priest. "Were you any good?"

"I had an excellent teacher," said Jesus, "and no customer ever complained about my work."

"So you felt that you were helping others through your work and harming no one?"

"Yes. I believe that is exactly what I felt."

"Tomorrow," said the priest, "we shall talk about Step Five of the eight-fold path. It involves the work that people do, and I believe you will find it most interesting."

"I agree wholeheartedly," said Jesus after the priest had introduced the basic teachings of Step Five. "Everyone must have an occupation that enables him to care for himself and help others. And what he does should absolutely not bring harm to anyone. I would have felt very badly if one of the chairs that I had built would have broken and caused harm to the person sitting on it."

"And, of course, that would not ever happen if you put the correct effort into your work," said the priest.

"Amen," said Jesus.

"Which brings us to Step Six which is Right Effort. And this refers not only to the occupation that a person follows but also to the way he lives his entire life."

"I see nothing wrong with Step Six so far," said Jesus.

"Right Effort means that we each have to try every day to eliminate any evil qualities that may be within us and take all precautions to keep new ones from cropping up."

"I'm all in favor of asking my Father in Heaven each day to help us resist all temptations and to help us avoid new dangers that are constantly cropping up both around us and within us."

"That is very handy for you to have a Father in Heaven whom you can ask for help as you try to lead a perfect life. As I have already said, Gautama did not teach of the existence of such an all-powerful God, but only how to experience the highest degree of consciousness that must exist in the perfect condition of Nirvana."

"I think that Gautama came very close to realizing the existence of my Father in Heaven," said Jesus. "He just could not bring himself to assign the name of God to him."

"That may be," said the priest. "But let us return to the Sixth Step. Right Effort also demands that each person not only develop the good and moral qualities he already possesses, but he must always try to acquire new ones. Each person must seek to grow in maturity and perfection until he experiences universal love"

"Universal love," repeated Jesus. "What a tremendous realization Gautama had with that statement."

"I take it that you wholly agree with it," said the priest.

"Absolutely! In fact, in my opinion, all of the laws and teachings handed down over the years by the prophets who shared the wisdom of my Father in Heaven with His people can be reduced to two guidelines based solidly on love."

"And what are your two guidelines?" asked the priest.

"Love your Father in Heaven with all your heart and soul and love your neighbor as yourself."

"I think that you and Gautama would have gotten along just fine," said the priest.

"Well, we would have had our differences, but I would have had a lot of respect for him. And I think I could have helped him add the name of God to his condition of Nirvana," said Jesus. "I believe he would have been grateful if I could have convinced him that his attainment of happiness does not have to rely entirely on self effort. If he had accepted the fact that my Father in Heaven loved and cared for him, he would have found much comfort in asking for the help he needed to achieve happiness."

When one has a friend with whom he looks forward to spending his days, time passes quickly and pleasantly. Before either of them knew it, many months had passed by the time the Buddhist priest was finally ready to share with Jesus the final two steps contained in the Fourth Noble Truth.

"The final two steps," began the priest, "are what I like to call the quiet steps."

"And why is that?" asked Jesus.

"Because they require pleasant, relaxed surroundings and absolute freedom from distractions. They are steps that require the total concentration of a person's mind," said the priest.

"I also place great importance on the need for quiet time and freedom from distraction," said Jesus. "I believe these conditions are necessary to contemplate the will of my Father in Heaven and to meditate on how best to execute His will here on earth. I always prefer to be alone and free from distractions when I pray to my Father in Heaven and share with Him my concerns, my needs and my gratitude for all of His daily help."

"Well, then," said the priest, "once again it seems that you will be in agreement with the teachings of Gautama."

"And what is the Seventh Step?" asked Jesus.

"Step Seven is Right Contemplation. To contemplate properly, a person must be absolutely free of distractions and yet be totally alert and observant. He must free himself of all sorrows and from the distractions of any desires. He must, therefore, be rested, healthy and properly nourished when he begins to contemplate so that he will be able to focus all of his thoughts on the attainment of the perfect existence known as Nirvana."

"Those are habits that I myself attempt to follow when I spend time daily in prayer," said Jesus. "Gautama has offered his followers very sound advice."

"And," said the priest, "Step Eight is very similar to Step Seven. It simply helps the student of Gautama to reach the final level."

"And what is Step Eight?"

"Step Eight is Right Meditation."

"And Gautama is obviously making a distinction between contemplation and meditation," said Jesus.

"Oh, a very important one," said the priest. "In fact, you could say the difference between the two is the difference between darkness and light. It is the difference between contentment and the absolute bliss of Nirvana. Moving from contemplation to correct and in-depth meditation can be a life-long journey for us. It is no easy task, but we believe that the rewards are absolutely worth it."

"Is there a simple explanation that is offered to one who begins to take the Eighth Step?" asked Jesus.

"After freeing himself from all the distractions that accompany an imperfect lifestyle, a person must focus his mind until he gets to the point where he is totally unaware of any sensations of pleasure or pain associated with his body. He will then be able to glide into a state of consciousness that transcends his physical bonds. At that point the person will enter the state of perfection, peace and eternal bliss that Gautama teaches us is Nirvana."

Jesus sat quietly for a long while as he thought about the explanation offered by the priest.

"Have you nothing to say about Step Eight," asked the priest finally.

"A state of Grace," said Jesus.

"A state of what?" asked the Buddhist priest.

"What Gautama is talking about is what I would call a state of Grace. It is a state of absolute peace and contentment that is offered us by our Father in Heaven when we comply absolutely with His will while we are living on earth."

"And you know those who experience this state of Grace?" asked the priest.

"I have known many holy individuals who have described the feeling in great detail," said Jesus.

"And what is the feeling of being in a state of Grace?"

"When one is in a state of Grace, he is not necessarily unaware of his physical body nor unaware of his surroundings. He does, however, experience complete peace and internal happiness. He is conscious of no discomfort, suffers no regrets, feels no guilt, harbors no ill-will toward others, but, on the contrary, is filled with a feeling of love for all around him," said Jesus.

"So your state of Grace seems to allow a person to attain the universal love that Gautama offered as a goal on the road to perfection," observed the priest.

"It would seem so," agreed Jesus.

Jesus continued to accept the hospitality of the Buddhist priest for a while longer before he became curious about other non-Buddhist practices that he saw being followed in the town in which the priest lived.

"I take it," said Jesus one day, "that not all of the people in your great country call themselves Buddhists."

"Oh," said the priest, "there are comparatively few of us when one considers the great antiquity and the very wide-spread acceptance of the most ancient religious beliefs throughout this country and other lands to the east."

"And what are those believers called?" asked Jesus.

"Most of those who follow those beliefs are called Saindavas[1] in their Sanskrit language or Hendavas according to an ancient Avesta language, and I would say that they worship a god similar to your Father in Heaven."

"I remember that you mentioned the word Saindava earlier when you began to speak about Gautama. Does it have a meaning?" asked Jesus.

"You have a very good memory, my friend," said the priest. "The word means a person who lives near the Sindhu or Indus River."

"And you believe that the Saindavas worship a god similar to my Father in Heaven?" asked Jesus.

"I believe so. They believe that their high god was the creator of all things."

"And what do they call their high god?" asked Jesus.

"They call him Brahma," said the priest.

"And as Buddhists," asked Jesus, "do you believe you have nothing in common with the beliefs of the Saindavas?"

"Well, I wouldn't say that we have nothing in common," objected the priest.

"Are there beliefs that you share with them?"

"There is one concept that we seem to share," said the priest.

"What is that?"

"It is the Saindava concept of ultimate reality, a condition they call Brahman—not to be confused with their word for the creator, Brahma."

"What do they understand the condition of Brahman to be?" asked Jesus.

"Well, Brahman seems to refer to an impersonal world spirit that is identical with the souls of individual believers. It is when Brahman is described as a condition of Being, Consciousness and Bliss that it seems to resemble the condition of Nirvana for which we Buddhists strive."

"The fact that they believe in a Creator would seem to give them something in common with the Israelites also," observed Jesus.

"Perhaps," said the priest. "Do the scriptures of the Israelites identify a time when your Creator made the heavens and the earth?"

"Yes," said Jesus.

"And is there a time suggested when the Creator will call those He has created back to Himself?"

"Yes," said Jesus.

"Then I am afraid that you will find there are great differences in your ideas about your Creators."

"Why is that?" asked Jesus.

"Because the priests of Brahma—men who are called Brahamanas—teach that their God has created a universe that is unimaginably immense in size and duration, and that it is a universe that is passing through a continuous process of development and decline. The Brahamanas discuss cycles of time that are hundreds and hundreds of thousands of years long."

"And how does a Saindava view his life among these cycles?" asked Jesus.

"A Saindava considers existence to be a vale of tears and suffering—the same suffering that we Buddhists seek to avoid by striving for Nirvana. He believes that he is destined to remain involved in the long duration of the universe by passing through a long series of birth, death and rebirth cycles until he is finally born again into his salvation."

"Now that, my friend," said Jesus, "is indeed interesting."

"What is?" asked the priest.

"It is interesting that a Saindava believes that he will attain salvation by being born again. This is precisely a message I intend to share with God's people when I return to Judea."

"I'm not sure I understand what you mean," said the priest.

"The people of my Father in Heaven have been living for many years following the directives of His prophets and the early laws passed on by my Father in Heaven to Moses. Those laws and directives were intended to get His people to a certain point so they would be ready to accept the Salvation that He has prepared for them."

"And are they now ready to receive that Salvation?" asked the priest.

"They will be as soon as I return to offer it to them."

"Why you?"

"Because I am the Son of my Father in Heaven whom He has sent to be with His people. I am Immanuel. I am their Messiah. I have come to offer them Salvation."

The Buddhist priest looked intently at Jesus and was captivated by the sincerity and passion of his declarations. The thought crossed his mind that his guest and student was indeed a very special person, one, perhaps, whose importance he was not in a position to appreciate fully.

"And how will the people of your God be able to accept the Salvation you have been sent to offer?" asked the priest.

"They will need to be born again," said Jesus. "They will need to set aside their old lives and accept new ones. The new life will not be motivated by fear and legalistic regulations, but by forgiveness and love."

"And this Salvation will be available to all of your God's people?" asked the priest.

"To all who believe in me and go to the Father through me."

"I see," said the priest.

"And now, my friend," said Jesus with a sparkle in his eye and a warm smile on his face, "I need one more favor from you before I leave your home and generous hospitality."

"So soon?" asked the priest. "There is much more that we could discuss, and I have many more questions I wish to ask of you."

"I'm afraid that I really must be continuing my travels at this time. If you pray to my Father in Heaven as I have taught you, you will find all the answers you seek," consoled Jesus. "And now may I ask a final favor?"

"Name your favor, and I shall freely grant it if it is within my power," said the priest.

"I believe that before I begin my return journey home, I would like to learn more about the very ancient beliefs in Brahma that you say are widespread throughout this great land and through the lands to the east. Can you introduce me to a Saindava who would be as patient a teacher as you have been?" asked Jesus.

"I believe I can. There is a wise and patient Saindava who lives with his family on a small farm. I once enjoyed his generous hospitality during my own travels, and I feel sure you would be equally welcome. In fact, if you like, I will even accompany you to his house."

"I shall look forward to traveling with you," said Jesus.

"And now," said the priest, "let us get some rest. We will have a long journey ahead of us."

---

[1] *The Saindavas or Hendavas were the people that would later become known to the Persians as the Hindos or Hindus.*

Chapter 11

Jesus as a Guest in a Hindu Household

Jesus and the Buddhist priest had journeyed for several days to reach the farm, and on the last day, since they were getting very close, they decided just to keep on going as it grew dark rather than stopping to sleep. When they finally reached the house, it was just past the middle of the night.

"I'll knock and call his name," said the priest. "He'll recognize my voice."

"Kabir," called the priest. "Kabir, can you hear me?"

At first there was no reply, so the priest knocked again, this time a little harder.

"Kabir. Kabir, wake up. I have come to visit you."

"Is that you, my Buddhist friend?" finally came a sleepy but friendly reply.

"Yes, Kabir. It is I. I'm sorry to wake you, but a friend and I have traveled through the night to reach your house, and we have just now arrived."

"I'll be right there," said Kabir and then called to his wife. "Mira, we have guests who have been traveling all through the night to get here. You must get up and fix something to eat."

Mira arose immediately and, as she was getting dressed to meet their company, she suddenly realized that there was not enough bread in the house to offer guests.

"Kabir, there was only enough bread left last night for our breakfast. I was going to bake more the first thing in the morning. What shall we do?"

"Don't worry. Fix whatever else we have, and I will run to our neighbor and borrow some from him. Keep our guests company until I return."

As soon as Kabir was dressed, he hurried to the door and welcomed his old friend and his traveling companion.

"Welcome, Welcome. It is good to see you again. And who is your friend?" said Kabir.

"This is Jesus who has traveled from Judea to visit our lands. He and I have spent much time together since he was interested in learning about my beliefs and practices."

"He could have no better teacher," said Kabir.

"And now," said the priest, "I have brought him to you because I know that you, too, will have the patience to share your religious beliefs and practices with him. You will find him to be pleasant and very helpful. And he is an excellent student."

"You are both welcome," said Kabir. "Will you be staying with us also?"

"No," replied the priest. "It is my intention to begin my return trip home in the morning. I just wanted to accompany him to your house and have the pleasure of seeing you and your family again."

"Come in, and sit," said Kabir.

"Mira!" called the priest as soon as he saw Kabir's wife at the kitchen table. "How are you, and how are the children?"

"We are fine. We are all fine. Please come and sit. Kabir is going to run to our neighbor's house and borrow some bread, and then we shall all have a bite to eat."

As Jesus and the priest settled around the table and began to chat with Mira, Kabir left and headed for his neighbor's house. As he drew near, he saw that the house was completely dark. He also knew that his neighbor could be a little grumpy when disturbed, but he felt sure he would loan him three loaves of bread which he would pay back after his wife baked in the morning.

"Friend!" called Kabir beneath his neighbor's bedroom window. "Friend, wake up. It's Kabir, your neighbor. I need your help."

There was no response.

"Hello!" called Kabir more loudly. "Please wake up, my friend. It is I, Kabir, your neighbor."

After a while, a curtain moved at the window, and a sleepy head emerged.

"Don't you know it's the middle of the night?" said the neighbor in a hoarse voice.

"I know, and I'm sorry to bother you," said Kabir.

"Then go away."

"But, Neighbor," persisted Kabir, "an old friend of mine has come from a long journey and I have no bread to set before him."

"Look," said the neighbor, beginning to be irritated, "my door is locked for the night and my children are in bed with us. I can't get up to give you any bread."

"But," said Kabir, "if you could just let me have three loaves, Mira will be baking in the morning and we shall pay you back immediately."

"Go home, and quit bothering me," said the neighbor whose head suddenly disappeared behind the curtains.

Kabir, however, was not about to give up.

"Friend," called Kabir again, "when have I ever refused to help you when you asked. I know it's late, but this is a very special friend who has brought a guest from Judea and we must have some bread to offer them. They have been traveling all night long to reach my house, and we have only a few scraps of bread. All I need is three loaves. I'll pay you back six loaves tomorrow if you wish. Please, come down and open the door."

"Do you persist?" came an even grouchier voice from behind the curtain.

"Just go down and give him three loaves," said a female voice in the background. "If you don't, we'll never get any sleep tonight."

"Please," said Kabir. "As soon as I have the loaves I need, I will leave you to your rest."

All was silent for a while, and Kabir was just about ready to repeat his pleas when he heard the door being unbolted.

"Come in," said the neighbor after he had opened the door. "There's the bread. Take what you need."

"Thank you," said Kabir. "You are a true friend."

"I'm not giving them to you because you're my friend," grumbled the neighbor. "Only because you've made a total pest of yourself."

"Thank you anyway," said Kabir. "I shall send one of our children over tomorrow to repay you."

"Just let me get back to sleep," rasped the neighbor who quickly relocked the door as soon as Kabir left.

The next day, the Buddhist priest took his leave as planned and left Jesus to settle in with his new host family.

Mira went right to work with her oldest daughter baking bread. Jesus watched as three measures of flour were heaped on a large table.

"That's a lot of flour!" said the girl when she saw that her Mom had poured a whole bushel of flour out for her to work with.

"We have to make extra bread today," said the Mother. "We need to take bread to our neighbor, plus we have company!"

The daughter was then told to get a small amount of yeast from its container.

"Want to see some magic?" asked the girl of Jesus.

"Why sure," said Jesus. "What trick do you have?"

"Well, do you see this little bit of yeast?"

"Yes," said Jesus.

"And do you see how big the pile of flour is that's on the table?"

"Yes. I watched your mother pour three measures of flour down for you. It certainly is a big pile!"

"Well, the trick is that this little bit of yeast will double the size of the flour once a little water is added and it's all mixed up."

Jesus watched as the girl's strong arms began kneading the flour and working the water and yeast throughout the mixture. When she finished, Jesus helped her form the dough into a huge ball, which she then covered with a cloth.

"It is still the same size," said Jesus.

"Well, of course it is, Silly," said the girl. "We have to give the yeast some time to work. But you'll see. If you come back after while, the ball of dough will be twice as big as it is now."

"And then what will you do?" asked Jesus.

"Then I'll flatten it all down again and begin shaping it into small loaves."

Then, turning to her mother, she asked, "Mom, how many loaves do you think I'll be able to make?"

"About sixteen," said her mother.

"And then?" asked Jesus.

"Then the magic will work a second time."

"Really?" asked Jesus.

"Yes," said the girl. "Each of the loaves will grow twice as big again before we bake them in the oven outside."

"You are a very smart girl," said Jesus.

"Oh, my mother taught me that trick when I was little. But I still love to watch it happen whenever we bake bread."

"And, Mira," said Kabir, "be sure to have our son wait until later in the afternoon to take the six loaves to our neighbor. I want to be sure he's is well rested after last night."

It didn't take Jesus many days to learn that Kabir was, indeed, a very intelligent and patient head of his household, and, as the priest had predicted, he sincerely appreciated having Jesus as his guest.

One the first things that Jesus noticed as he settled in were the careful and solemn home-based religious rituals that were part of family life. Each day the children would gather wild flowers which their mother would place before a sacred image displayed on a small cupboard. Mira would then lead the children in a sacred song while lighting incense before the image.

There was also a careful ritual that accompanied the family's evening meal. Kabir was definitely the head of the family and, similar to the Jewish traditions of Jesus, he led the family's evening meal religious rituals. As Jesus watched each evening, Kabir would dedicate a portion of the food as sort of a ritualistic sacrifice to his god. He would then take a cup into which a powerful drink called Soma had been poured and, after symbolically offering its contents to his god, would drink the liquid.

After each evening meal, Kabir would gather his family around him and take copies of their sacred scrolls out of a container. His sons would then be asked to recite by heart passages they had been studying, and the whole family would listen as Kabir and his oldest son took turns reading new passages from the scrolls.

This, too, reminded Jesus of the evenings he, as a young boy, had spent studying the sacred scrolls with Joseph in his home in Nazareth.

To ease his burden on the family, Jesus insisted that he be allowed to help Kabir with the farm work. Kabir appreciated his help, and before long a whole month had passed.

"I love farming," said Kabir one day. "It always amazes me how the seeds grow after I have sown them."

"I know," said Jesus. "While we sleep and go about our business, they grow."

"And before you know it," continued Kabir, "you look out and see the ground green with the first blades that rise above the earth. I have to watch to make sure insects, birds or weeds don't overrun them, but other than that, they seem to know what they are doing."

"And before long," added Jesus, "the seeds have produced ears full of grain."

"And that's when my work begins," said Kabir. "That's when it's time to sharpen the sickle and begin the harvest."

"Do your neighbors worship the same sacred image which you honor in your home?" asked Jesus one day as he was working in a field beside his host.

"Oh, no," replied Kabir. "Almost everyone has a different sacred image."

"But don't all Saindavas worship the same god, Brahma?" asked Jesus.

"Brahma is our high god, the creator of all things," said Kabir, "but there are many, many gods that are worshipped by those who believe in Brahma."

"How many?" asked Jesus.

"Well, they can't really be counted because we believe that all people and objects are partly divine and are, in a way, little gods. It is because of this shared divinity that we believe that children owe divine respect to their parents, that wives owe divine respect to their husbands, students to their teachers, the young to the aged, religious followers to their priests. We even believe that a workman owes divine respect to his tools, and that we all owe divine respect to the food and drink that we enjoy each day."

"Are you talking about respect or about a whole bunch of different gods?" asked Jesus.

"I'm talking about a whole bunch of different gods. People throughout this land and the lands to the east worship more gods than can be counted," said Kabir.

"But the God of my people," said Jesus, "insists that His people have no other gods before Him."

"And our god, Brahma, has stated that whatever god a man worships, it is he, Brahma, who answers their prayers," countered Kabir.

"You would seem to have a very tolerant and open-minded god," said Jesus. "Are your religious guidelines also lax?"

"On the contrary," insisted Kabir. "The guidelines of our religion are very precise and strict. There are great scrolls, called Vedas, in which are carefully recorded complex and precise guidelines which govern all the actions of the members of the top levels of our society."

"How many levels are there?" asked Jesus.

"There are four," replied Kabir. "Those in the lowest level are left more unrestricted until they can earn their entrance into one of the top three levels and begin their quest of salvation."

"And how does one earn his entrance into a higher level?"

"By being born again," replied Kabir.

"Ah, yes," said Jesus. "By being born again. I had heard that from our friend, the Buddhist priest."

On another day, as Jesus accompanied Kabir into the fields to work, he noticed a half built tower on a nearby hill. Since there was no evidence of ongoing work on the tower, Jesus asked Kabir about it.

"Is that tower in the distance being torn down or built?" asked Jesus.

"Neither," said Kabir. "It was being built, but it has now been abandoned."

"And why is that?" asked Jesus.

"Well, it was supposed to be a watch tower that one of my neighbors wanted to build so he could look out and inspect all of his fields without having to travel to see them up close."

"Why did he abandon the project?" asked Jesus.

"Poor planning," said Kabir. "He laid in the foundation and had enough stone to build what you see, and then he realized that he did not have enough funds to finish the project. After that, he had several poor years and eventually was forced to sell the fields he had intended to use the tower to watch. So there it sits."

"That is sad," said Jesus. "But, you know, not only farmers and builders need to plan ahead. Even wealthy kings must follow the same advice."

"How is that?" asked Kabir.

"Well," continued Jesus, "Let's say that one king intends to go to war with another. When such a king catches sight of his enemy, he must carefully consider whether or not he can win."

"And if he decides that he can't?" asked Kabir.

"Then it is only wise that he send envoys while there is still time so they can seek peace rather than risk the ruin of his entire army."

"You are right, my friend," agreed Kabir. "Do you realize that there are some who not only never learn to plan ahead but who don't even know how to read the signs of nature so they can be ready for what will happen next."

"Have you learned to read the signs of nature?" asked Jesus.

"I believe so," said Kabir, "or else I would not be able to farm successfully. For instance, do you see that fig tree just ahead?"

"Yes," said Jesus.

"Well, it tells me that summer is near," said Kabir. "When the branch of the fig tree is tender and begins to sprout leaves, that's how I know that summer is coming."

"You're right," agreed Jesus. "If a man is wise, he will see the signs of things to come."

"Look over there," said Kabir. "See that other fig tree?"

"The one to the left of that large rock?" asked Jesus.

"Yes. That one I think I might as well cut down."

"Why?"

"It hasn't had any figs on it for the past three years. It's just taking up space as far as I'm concerned."

"I tell you what," said Jesus. "Let me cultivate it a little for you and work in some manure while I'm here."

"Do you think that will help?" asked Kabir.

"I think it will," said Jesus. "But if it still doesn't have any figs, then you might as well go ahead and cut it down."

Over the weeks and months that Jesus stayed with Kabir, their conversations continued as Kabir answered all of Jesus' questions, and Jesus shared personal information about his own life and his mission as Immanuel among the people of his Father in Heaven.

Jesus was interested to learn that just as Gautama had set out Four Noble Truths to lead his followers to Nirvana, those who worshipped Brahma believed that there were four stages of life that were to be lived by members of the top three levels of society. Instead of an eight-fold path leading to Nirvana, however, Kabir explained that there were only three rules of conduct that each man must follow to attain his personal Moksha or salvation.

But the thing that most impressed Jesus as he listened to Kabir's detailed and careful explanations was that Kabir was not insisting, as the Buddhist priest had done, that all desires were bad and needed to be eliminated before true happiness could be attained. A point of view that was much more in keeping with the beliefs of Jesus was Kabir's insistence that the ideal life for a man needed to be based on a middle of the road approach. It was almost as though Kabir and the other Saindavas had come across the Greek notion of "Nothing in Excess." This was a refreshing change.

"You love Mira very much, don't you?" asked Jesus as he and Kabir were heading out for their daily chores one day.

"We are one," said Kabir, very matter-of-factly. "We believe that our love for each other is everlasting and that our marriage is indissoluble."

"What if you were to die?" asked Jesus. "Would Mira be free to marry again so she could have help raising the children?"

"Absolutely not. A wife is eternally bound by marriage to her husband. In fact, my friend, if you stay with us long enough, you may witness a funeral at which a dead man's widow will hurl herself upon her departed husband's pyre. You see, it will be her belief that she has no further existence without her husband."

"Your dedication to the bond of marriage is indeed impressive," said Jesus. "Very impressive."

"Then you seem to agree with our view of marriage," observed Kabir.

"Yes and No," said Jesus, smiling in friendship.

"Please explain."

"Well, I agree that no man should separate those whom God has joined together, but I don't believe it is right for a widow to kill herself when her husband dies. But now," said Jesus, choosing to change the subject, "I would like to hear about the four stages of life that you say are open to those who belong to the three highest levels of your society."

"Well, we believe that one must start with an initiation that we call Upanayana."

"And when does this occur?" asked Jesus.

"Just before a boy reaches puberty," said Kabir.

"And that is when the young man enters the first stage of his life?" asked Jesus.

"Yes. That is when he becomes a Brahmachari, which is our name for a celibate student. During this stage of his life he will devote himself entirely to his studies and learn all that he must know to be the head of a family of his own one day. He is to give no thought to girls because his father will have already arranged for a girl whom he will marry."

"And when he marries, is that when he enters the second stage of his life?" asked Jesus.

"Yes. When he marries, he becomes a Grihastha, the head of his household. This will be the most important part of his life. If he has been properly prepared, he will be able to follow the middle road in all of his dealings."

"And what guidelines are there for him during this important part of his life?" asked Jesus.

"His studies will have taught him that there are three guidelines of personal conduct that he must follow to achieve salvation or Moksha," said Kabir.

"And these are?"

"The first is most important and takes precedent over the two that follow. This we call Dharma. It means that in all his actions he must strive to be righteous and act with religious merit."

"That is a sound code of conduct for any man," agreed Jesus.

"We call the second code of conduct Artha. Artha dictates that the young man must strive for profit and material advantage in all of his dealings so that he can provide as well as possible for his family. To achieve Artha a man must be clever, resourceful and persistent in his dealings and yet be always governed by Dharma and act with religious merit."

"That would seem to be a very great challenge," observed Jesus.

120

"Very great indeed!"

"And the third code of conduct to be followed while the young man is living as a Grihastha?" asked Jesus.

"The third is called Kama. Kama dictates that a man must learn to enjoy his life. Pleasure is a great reward given us by Brahma. If a person is living his life correctly, pleasure will follow from his activities."

"And, of course, this must be where the caution to follow the middle road becomes most important," observed Jesus.

"It is in following Kama that most men lose sight of the first and most important code of conduct," said Kabir.

"That a man must be righteous and be motivated by religious merit," said Jesus.

"It is no easy task," said Kabir.

"Have you known men who have become very wealthy and yet have not found happiness?" asked Jesus.

"Yes. And that is very sad when that happens," said Kabir. "In fact, not too many years ago, one of my neighbors seemed to be enjoying his life to the fullest as dictated by Kama. That year, he could see that his fields were going to produce more grain than they ever had before."

"Did he have room to store it all?" asked Jesus.

"That was a problem. So he immediately hired a crew to tear down his old barns and build new, bigger barns. And it had to work fast so the barns would be ready by the time the harvest began."

"Did the crew finish on time?" asked Jesus.

"Oh, that was no problem. The barns were built and the harvest was being laid in. That's when he invited the rest of us over to his house for a great celebration. He said that as far as he was concerned, he was set for years to come and that we shouldn't worry if we saw that he wasn't working his fields for a few years. He was going to take it easy, eat, drink and be merry."

"And what happened to him that was so sad?" asked Jesus.

"He died. That very night. We all heard about it the next day. It was very sad."

"It often happens that way," said Jesus, "with those who lay up treasures for themselves here on earth and neglect their Father in Heaven."

"And we all thought he was doing so well," said Kabir.

"And what is the third stage of life open to a man in the upper classes?" asked Jesus.

"The third stage is called Vana Prastha. This is the stage a man enters when he has become a grandparent. The guidelines for this stage suggest that he move into a small hut in the country and become a spiritual recluse. He should plan to care for himself and not be a burden on his children."

"And the fourth stage to which a man must look forward?" asked Jesus.

"When a man becomes very old, he becomes a Sannyasi. In this stage he must resign himself to living as a homeless religious beggar, depending on the pious generosity of others for his existence."

"That would seem to be a way of life that would require great faith in the generosity of others," said Jesus.

"Of course. But you must remember, my friend," said Kabir, "that those who are younger will recognize the divinity in a Sannyasi and generously offer him respect and support."

While Jesus was a guest on the farm of Kabir and Mira, he had many opportunities to take part in a number of festivals that were held at different times of the year. It was during these festival times that he had a chance to spend time with their children, something he sincerely enjoyed. He loved to hear their views on life and nature and their clever explanations of things that they were not yet old enough to understand fully. And just as Jesus loved to hear stories when he was young, he also enjoyed sharing them with the children.

As it happened, the time for the end of the year harvest festivals came while Jesus was at the home of Kabir and Mira. The celebrations that were enjoyed reminded him of those called Saturnalia that he had observed Roman settlers in Judea celebrate.

Jesus took this opportunity to explain to the children the Hebrew festival of Hannukah. He told them how the Jewish people were once imprisoned and forbidden to study or discuss their sacred scrolls which they called the Torah.

After sharing these stories with the children, Jesus spent a little time carving a small dreidel out of a piece of scrap wood. When he next met with the children, he explained how the Hebrew prisoners made a similar spinning top from clay and used it secretly to continue their discussions of the Torah.

The children of Kabir and Mira were, of course, fascinated by the new toy.

"What are the marks on each side of the dreidel?" asked Kabir's oldest son who knew how to read Sanskrit.

"They are Hebrew letters," explained Jesus. "Each is the first letter of a word."

"What are the words?" asked one of the little girls, full of playful curiosity.

"This letter," began Jesus patiently, "is nun. It is the first letter of the Hebrew word 'new' which means 'miracle.' "

"And the others?" asked the oldest son.

"This is gimmel, the first letter of the word 'gadol' that means 'great,' and this is hey. It stands for the word 'haya' which means 'was.' The last letter is shin, and it stands for the word 'sham' which means 'there.' Now," said Jesus playfully, "who can put all the words together to see what they say?"

The eldest of Kira's daughters spoke up immediately.

"The words 'gadol nex haya sham' mean 'a great miracle was there!' "

"Ve-ry good!" said Jesus, amazed at the excellent memory and quickness of the young girl. "And now, who would like to play a little game?"

"We would!" said all the children in unison.

"Okay," said Jesus, as he produced a small bowl filled with five dates for each child. "Each of you take five dates from the bowl, but don't eat them. They are going to be the prizes."

Jesus watched as each child carefully counted out five dates and placed them in neat piles. He then set the empty bowl in the center of their little circle.

"Now," said Jesus, "each of you must place one date in the bowl, and then you will take turns spinning the dreidel to see if you can win the dates in the bowl."

"How do we win?" asked the youngest girl.

"After you spin the dreidel, it will fall on one of its sides. We will then look at the letter that is facing upwards. If the letter is nun, you win nothing and the next person gets to spin. If the letter facing upwards is gimel, you win all the dates in the bowl and then we start all over again. But if the letter heh is on top, you only get to take half of the dates in the bowl."

"What happens if the letter shin is facing upwards?" asked the oldest boy.

"Then you have to add one date to the bowl before the next person spins the dreidel," explained Jesus.

Jesus loved spending time with the children, and they, in turn, were naturally drawn to him whenever they had time free from their chores.

Although there was no temple in the area where Jesus was staying—and none was missed since most of the religious observances of his hosts were based in their home—Jesus did learn that temples did exist, especially in larger cities.

"Have you ever met any of those who devote their entire lives to the worship of Brahma?" asked Jesus one day.

"No, but I have heard that some of them lead lives of great personal sacrifice and become very holy."

"Great personal sacrifice?" asked Jesus.

"They own nothing throughout their lives and depend entirely on the food that is offered them by others."

"A very admirable lifestyle," said Jesus, "one which I, too, attempt to follow."

"They say," continued Kabir, "that one particular holy man lived a life of such self-denial and prayer that he was able to achieve great supernatural powers."

"Powers to do what?" asked Jesus recalling his experiences with the priest of Sekhmet in Egypt.

"Powers to heal the sick, make the deaf hear and the blind see."

"Very impressive," said Jesus. "Very impressive."

"Those who saw him work these wonders became ever more dedicated to the worship of Brahma from whom the holy man's powers seemed to come."

"As one would expect," said Jesus. "Exactly as one would expect. I have seen wonder-workers draw followers in exactly the same way during my visit to Egypt."

When the day came for Jesus to take his leave of Kabir and Mira and begin his 1,500-mile journey back to Nazareth, Kabir said he wanted to read a special prayer for Jesus, one that he hoped would comfort him in his long journey.

"And what is the prayer?" asked Jesus.

"I will say it first in very old Sanskrit so you can hear its beauty. Then my oldest son will translate it for you."

And so, after first solemnly setting the mood and gathering his family around their departing guest, Kabir began the prayer. When he finished all sat silently for a moment.

"Those were indeed beautiful sounding words," said Jesus. "And their meaning?"

Kabir smiled and invited his oldest son to offer a translation to their departing guest.

> "May the Lord lead you from the unreal to the real.
> May he lead you from the darkness to light.
> May he lead you from death to immortality.
> May there be peace, peace and perfect peace."

"And may the peace of my Father in Heaven be with you and all your family," said Jesus as he took his leave.

"And also with you," said Kabir and his family in unison.

Chapter 12

Jesus Begins his 1,500 Mile Journey back to Judea

The 1,500-mile journey back to Judea would take Jesus nearly a half a year. He was in such excellent physical condition that he could have completed the trip in 60 or 80 days, but he believed in stopping occasionally and spending time with those who offered him food and hospitality along the way. He enjoyed sharing the lives and stories of his hosts and offering them what wisdom and consolation they were ready to accept.

The area through which Jesus was now traveling was not always the best farmland. He came across many families that were trying to survive by sowing whatever seeds they could save from year to year. Most were families who simply sowed their seeds randomly and hoped for some sort of harvest.

One of the first couples with whom he stayed for a few days lived in a very simple hillside structure built of stone with a sloping thatched roof.

As Jesus approached the stone structure, he saw a little old man stooped over weeding a small vegetable garden with his hoe.

"Peace," said Jesus when he got close enough to be heard.

The little old man stopped what he was doing and, leaning on the handle of his hoe for support, slowly straightened his body and looked in the direction of the greeting. He looked at Jesus for a while before a warm, welcoming smile came over his face.

"And peace with you, traveler. Are you lost?"

"Why no," said Jesus. "Why would you think that I am lost?"

"Because the only people who usually visit us are those who have lost their way in these hills," said the little old man.

"I am just passing through the area on my way to Judea," explained Jesus. "When I saw you working in your garden, I thought I would take time to wish you the peace of my Father in Heaven."

"Well, then, I'm glad that you did. Welcome! My name is Abbas."

"And I am Jesus."

"Come! Let us go inside and get out of the hot sun."

As they approached the door to the stone structure, Abbas called to his wife.

"Anaitis. We have a guest who is not lost. His name is Jesus."

"Oh Abbas, I wish you had warned me. I have not yet swept the floor today. But, no matter. Welcome, Jesus. Come and sit and have some cool water to drink."

As Jesus and Abbas sat at the table, Anaitis went right to work cleaning vegetables, cutting them up and putting them into a pot of boiling water that hung suspended near the hearth.

"Have you lived here long?" asked Jesus.

"All our married lives," said Anaitis.

"Nearly forty years," added Abbas. "But it doesn't seem that long. The years go by quickly when one has work for his hands and someone with whom to share his happiness."

"Have you no children to help you?" asked Jesus.

"We were never blessed with children," said Anaitis.

"But that has not prevented us from enjoying our life together," added Abbas. "We've had to work a little harder and share the jobs, but we are content."

"For two simple old people such as we are, it is more than we could have hoped for when we were young," added Anaitis.

"But enough about us," said Abbas. "Have you been traveling long?"

"Almost ten years," said Jesus. "But now I am happy to be on my way home."

"And where is your home?" asked Anaitis.

"I live in a small city in Judea called Nazareth."

"Can you rest with us for a couple of days?" asked Abbas.

"If it would not be an imposition," said Jesus.

"We would be most happy to have you as our guest. We get so few visitors," said Anaitis.

And so Jesus accepted the hospitality of the elderly couple, and once again offered to help with whatever work was being done during his stay.

"Today I was planning to sow some wheat in that area north of here in case you want to come along," said Abbas.

"Of course I'll come along," said Jesus.

Since the sack of seed was fairly large, Jesus offered to carry it for his elderly host.

"Won't we need a rake or a hoe to prepare the soil?" asked Jesus.

"Not on that piece of land," said Abbas. "The soil is too hard and rocky. I usually just scatter the seeds around. What grows, grows."

"And you have sown the seeds the same way in the past?" asked Jesus.

"Every year. Some seeds just fall on top of the ground and get eaten by the birds. Others fall in what little dirt there is around the rocks. Those seeds tend to sprout quickly, but I've learned not to get too excited about them. They usually just dry up and die in a couple of days. Not enough moisture. The heat from the rocks dries it all up."

"Do all the rest of the seeds give you a good crop?" asked Jesus.

"Not all of them. You can't see them now, but in some places where it looks like the soil is good, there are also a lot of thorn bush seeds waiting to sprout. They'll start growing about the same time, and any of my wheat seeds that lie near them won't have a chance."

"Then why do you keep sowing your seeds in that field?" asked Jesus

"Well, it might not sound like such a good idea," said Abbas, "but where the soil is good, and where there aren't a lot of thorn bush seeds, the wheat does very well. Some years I get anywhere from sixty to a hundredfold return on what I sow."

"Without having to spend a lot of time breaking up the soil or removing the rocks first," observed Jesus.

"You're absolutely right," said Abbas. "And besides, these old bones just don't have it in them any more to do that kind of heavy work."

After a few days, Jesus thanked the elderly couple and announced that he had to be moving on. He explained that he still had a very long journey ahead of him and that he had promised to return home before the end of the year.

As Jesus walked away from the cabin and turned to give a final smile and wave at his hosts, he thought to himself, "Blessed indeed are the meek and gentle for they shall surely inherit the earth."

Much of the time Jesus walked alone. He didn't mind it, though. He liked to have time to pray, to think and to consider all that he had seen and heard on his travels. He was beginning to make stories out of his experiences that he would be able to use when sharing his Good News.

With the help of travelers he did occasionally meet, Jesus was able to plan his route so that he would be able to obtain water at least once a day, either from a river or stream, or in very dry stretches, at an oasis. Of course, there would be many days when he would have to go without food, but he was used to fasting. On some days he came across a settlement, an occasional town or city, and even a small shepherd or goatherd lean-to where he would be welcomed.

Jesus was several months into his return trip when he happened to come into a fertile valley dominated by what looked to be a wealthy estate. Near the buildings of the estate there was a small vineyard, but most of the land contained either olive trees or fields planted with wheat. Since it would not be out of his way, Jesus decided to take time to meet the owner of the estate who, perhaps, would offer him some much welcomed hospitality.

As Jesus drew near, he was observed by an impressive looking man giving instructions to a small group of workers. The man would occasionally look up at Jesus as he told the workers what tasks he expected them to complete that day. By the time Jesus drew near enough to be addressed, the man had dismissed the workers and was patiently waiting to talk to Jesus.

"Greetings, Traveler," said the impressive looking man.

"May the peace of our Father in Heaven be with you," said Jesus and smiled in a way that immediately won the man over.

"And also with you," said the man, returning a friendly smile and offering Jesus his arm in friendship. "Have you traveled far?"

"Very far," said Jesus. "I have come from across the Indus River and am now on the final leg of my journey home."

"And where is home?"

"My home is in Nazareth, a small town north of Jerusalem in Judea," said Jesus.

"Ah, yes," said the man. "I know Judea. And how long have you been away from home?"

"When I return with the help of my Father in Heaven, I will have been gone nearly ten years," replied Jesus.

"Well," said he man, "let me welcome you to my estate. My name is Munir. I would be honored to have you rest with us a few days before you continue your journey." Then, noticing that Jesus carried nothing with him, he added, "You travel light. Don't you carry a pack or extra supplies with you?"

"I carry nothing except the clothes on my back and the sandals on my feet," said Jesus.

Munir glanced at the sandals Jesus was wearing and noticed that they were very worn, but said nothing.

"And how do you manage to eat and drink each day?"

"I make do with what I find along the road and with what is offered me by those I meet. My Father in Heaven has never failed to provide for me."

"Well," said Munir, "for as long as you would care to stay on my estate, I shall be glad to provide for you. Come, let us go to the house and get out of the sun."

As they walked along, Jesus asked his host about his crops and his olive trees and explained that in his travels he had worked beside several farmers to thank them for their hospitality. As they passed a wheat field that seemed also to be full of weeds, Jesus asked about the unusual sight.

"That was a perfectly good field," explained Munir. "Last year there were no weeds in it, and the yield of wheat was abundant."

"How did all the weeds get in it this year?" asked Jesus.

"Well, my friend," said Munir, "no man can become successful without making a few enemies. Even though I make every effort to be honest and fair in all of my dealings with my neighbors, there are always those who simply become jealous. The only thing that my workers and I can figure is that after the field was prepared and sowed with wheat, one of my enemies must have come during the night and scattered the seeds of many weeds that he had no doubt been collecting for just such a purpose."

"Have you not thought to have your workers pull the weeds up?" asked Jesus.

"At first we did try to do that, but we found that in the process we were trampling the wheat, and, as we pulled the weeds, the tender spouts of wheat were also being destroyed."

"So what will you do now?" asked Jesus.

"Well, there seems to be enough moisture in the field, so I've decided to just let them both grow together. Then at harvest time I'll have my workers bundle the weeds and burn them so their seeds will be destroyed. Then we shall harvest the wheat."

"Very impressive solution," said Jesus. "Very impressive indeed."

When they reached the main house on the estate, Munir first called for water for Jesus and then took him to a private room where he could rest for a while before food would be prepared. Later, Jesus was introduced to Munir's wife and two daughters.

"You were not blessed with a son?" asked Jesus.

"Our son is dead," said Munir in a tone that indicated he preferred not to discuss it further in the presence of his family.

That evening when Munir invited Jesus to recline with him for the evening meal, a servant came forward and began to remove their sandals.

"I noticed," said Munir confidentially, "that your sandals are very worn."

"This is at least the twentieth pair that I have had since beginning my travels," said Jesus. "They are worn, but still comfortable."

"With your permission," said Munir, still speaking quietly so as not to embarrass Jesus, "I will have my servant make a new pair for you during the night if he can use the ones he is removing to get the right measurements."

"Why, thank you," said Jesus. "That's very generous of you."

The next day, Jesus was well rested and looked forward to accompaning his host as he began his rounds. He put on his new sandals and found that they fit perfectly. As they drew near to the small vineyard Jesus had seen the day before, he asked why his host did not have a larger one planted.

"What you see on the side of that hill is just a test planting of vines that I did several years ago," said Munir dismissively. "They yield very few grapes and they are so sour that they can't be eaten or made into wine that anyone would want to drink. I keep the vines only because the grapes can be fed to the pigs."

"So you are not really interested in having a larger vineyard then, are you?" said Jesus.

"Oh, I would love to have a large vineyard," said Munir. "In fact, several years ago I, too, traveled east of the Indus River from which you have come. While I was there I came across some vines that produced large and sweet grapes that were being made into a wine such as I had never tasted before. I immediately purchased a very large field in the same district that would be perfect for a vineyard. I then hired local workmen to plant starts from those same vines. I had men build a hedge around the vineyard to keep out grazing animals, and then I designed a large winepress along with a watchtower so that I could have a guard posted to insure that the grapes would not be stolen."

"Does that happen?" asked Jesus.

"Absolutely," insisted Munir. "They can clean a whole vineyard out in one night."

"So such a tower is a necessary precaution."

"Yes," said Munir. "When I was done, I rented the vineyard to local vinedressers with the understanding that I was to receive half of the wine that would be produced."

"Did your vineyard not work out?" asked Jesus.

"Well, as you know, it usually takes several years for new vines to begin producing their best grapes. But when the time came, I received news that the harvest was expected to be very plentiful."

"So, were you able to collect your share of the wine?" asked Jesus.

"Well," said Munir, "I tried. As soon as the time of the year came when I knew that the grapes would be pressed, I sent three of my servants to collect my share of the wine."

"What happened?" asked Jesus.

"Only one returned, empty handed and badly beaten," said Munir.

"What happened to the others?"

"The servant who was beaten told me that the vineyard renters killed one and stoned the other. It was just by luck that he was able to escape."

"So did you abandon the project?" asked Jesus.

"Absolutely not," said Munir. "I sent ten more servants with strict orders to be careful, but firm, in demanding what was my due. Unfortunately, they had no better luck. Only two survived to report back to me."

"Don't tell me," said Jesus. "Did you end up sending your son to deal with the renters?"

"Yes," said Munir with a tone of deep sadness. "When he didn't return within a reasonable amount of time, I gathered a band of armed men and prepared to go to the vineyard myself."

"Such a trip would take you away from your estate and your wife and daughters for a long while, wouldn't it?" asked Jesus.

"Especially considering the task I had ahead of me when I got there," said Munir.

"With no son to leave in charge," asked Jesus, "how did you insure that your estate would be properly managed in your absence?"

"Well, I had no choice but to make one of my servants Chief Steward in my absence. I didn't really trust the man, but he was the most competent of all those in my employ."

"I guess that was a risk you had to take," said Jesus.

"I did take some precautions so the steward wouldn't be able to ruin me entirely if my suspicions proved to be true," said Munir.

"What did you do?" asked Jesus.

"Since I was going to be leaving a large quantity of silver coins behind, I decided to entrust them to some of the other servants who were especially faithful even though none of them had the abilities needed to serve as steward. To one I gave 5,000 silver coins with instructions for him to care for them as he knew I would want him to. To another, I gave 2,000 silver coins. To a third I gave 1,000.

"So then you were ready to leave," concluded Jesus.

"Yes. And when I crossed the Indus River with my band of armed men, I learned that the renters had killed my son and were trying to claim the vineyard as their own by telling a local judge that I had no other heirs."

"Were you able to prevent that from happening?" said Jesus.

"Absolutely. By the time my men got done with them, those that survived fled and abandoned all claims to the vineyard. Then, before I returned home I leased the vineyard to new renters that I felt positive would keep our arrangement."

"Did they also prove to be unreliable?" asked Jesus.

"No, they were reliable," said Munir. "But my heart was no longer in it. After one good harvest I sent an agent with instructions to sell the vineyard. Having lost my only son, I no longer had any taste for the wine."

"So," said Jesus getting more and more caught up in the whole adventure, "how did your steward work out while you were gone?"

"He turned out to be less than reliable, as I had suspected. The man was selling everything on credit to his friends—oil, wheat, everything. In fact, if I hadn't placed my silver coins in the care of those others, I would have been completely ruined."

"So what did you do with him?" asked Jesus.

"I fired him, naturally. As far as I was concerned he could go out and dig ditches and beg for a living," said Munir.

"Is that what happened to him?"

"Not exactly," said Munir. "The man was clever. I have to give him credit for that at least."

"What did he do?"

"As soon as he left me, he paid a visit to everyone to whom he had sold oil, wheat and other things on credit and had them change their bills of sale."

"How?" asked Jesus.

"Well, to win their friendship and assure that he wouldn't be reduced to digging or begging to support himself, he told everyone who had bought a hundred jars of oil on credit to change their bills of sale to read fifty. Then he did the same thing with those who had bought a hundred bushels of wheat or anything else."

"At least he knew how to make friends, didn't he?" said Jesus.

"He was very clever," said Munir. "In fact, I actually congratulated him afterwards for knowing how to take care of himself. But, of course, I still fired him."

"I hope the servants with whom you left your silver coins proved to be more reliable," said Jesus.

"Pretty much so," said Munir. "At least none of them stole the coins. In fact, two of them even invested the coins I left in their care. When the servant to whom I had entrusted 5,000 silver coins showed me that he had turned his investment into 10,000, I was so impressed that I put him in charge of a good portion of my estate. When the second servant showed me that he had turned his 2,000 silver coins into 4,000, I also gave him a position of authority."

"What about the servant to whom you gave only 1,000 silver coins?" asked Jesus.

"He was a disappointment," said Munir. "He had simply hid his coins in a hole in the ground and then dug them up to return them to me. Of course, after he heard how wisely the others had invested their coins, he started trembling and babbling on and on. 'I knew you were a hard man,' he said, 'one who reaps where you don't sow and who gathers where you don't scatter, but I didn't want to take any chances with your coins. I knew I wouldn't be able to pay them back if I lost them on a bad investment, so I buried them. Here they are. You can count them. They're all there. None is missing. None is missing,' he kept insisting."

"So, what did you do with him?" asked Jesus.

"Well, I tell you," said Munir. "I let him have it. I called him every name in the book and told him that he should have at least entrusted his coins to the moneychangers so I could have gotten a little interest on them. Then I took his 1,000 and gave them to the servant who had made the best investment."

"The rich get richer," observed Jesus.

"And the poor get poorer," said Munir. "Of course, I didn't want him around anymore so I threw him off my estate. As far as I was concerned, he could just go off into the darkness, weeping and gnashing his teeth."

Jesus thought about all the things that Munir had shared with him and stored them up in his mind. He would give them more consideration as he continued his journey back to Judea.

On those days when Jesus neither found food growing near the road nor met other travelers who might share with him, he would have to fast. But his constitution was hardy, and he was always able to manage.

Since he was now beginning to draw closer to Judea, Jesus got into the habit of walking more hours each day, often not stopping to rest until it was dark. He also adjusted his route so that he would be able to pay a return visit to the widow he had met when he first started his trip. He was interested to see if she was able to obtain justice from her local judge.

One night, as he came over a small hill, he noticed a house below. The windows were dark, but there was a small group huddled before the front door, and several lamps were lit among them. At first, Jesus thought he would address the group and see if he might be offered food and lodging for the night. As he drew nearer, however, he saw that the group consisted of ten maidens and no men. Given the lateness of the hour, he decided that it would not be proper for him to seek hospitality from unescorted maidens. So, he located a spot under a comfortable tree and settled down for a rest.

Around midnight, Jesus was awakened by loud shouts and much excitement.

"He's coming! He's coming! Light your lamps. Hurry! We must run and light the road for him."

In the distance, a large wedding party led by the bridegroom and his new bride was making its way up the road. All those following were singing as they looked forward to continuing their celebration inside the home of the new couple.

After a while, the noise subsided, and Jesus could tell by the light shining from the windows of the house that the party had moved inside. He was just about to go back to sleep when he heard several maidens crying. Moved by compassion, he decided to see what was wrong.

"Peace," said Jesus as he drew near, not wanting to startle the five maidens that he saw huddled outside the closed door. "May I ask why all the crying?"

"We've been locked out of the wedding celebration," sobbed one.

"And we've been looking forward to it for such a long time," added another through her tears.

"And why have you been locked out?" asked Jesus.

"Well, we were all waiting here so we could welcome the bridegroom and light his way with our lanterns when he returned," explained one of the five, "but we five had not brought any extra oil for our lamps. We left them burning while we waited, and by the time the bridegroom finally came, our lamps had gone out."

"We tried," sobbed another, "to borrow oil from those that had extra, but they refused."

"So we all had to go to a neighbor's house and see if we could buy some lamp oil from him," said a third barely able to speak through her tears.

"Were you not able to obtain more oil for your lamps?" asked Jesus.

"Oh, we got the oil alright," said the first maiden who had spoken, "but by the time we got back, the whole wedding party had gone in, locking the door behind them."

"And now they won't let us in," cried yet another maiden. "The bridegroom claims he doesn't know who we are."

Jesus felt sorry for them, but he knew that he was not meant to interfere. As he returned to his tree to try and get a little more rest, he wondered whether the people of Israel would be watching and waiting for the arrival of their Messiah or whether many of them, too, would be left out of his Father's Kingdom in Heaven because they would not be properly prepared.

Several days later found Jesus approaching the small provincial town outside of which the house of the widow had been located. He hoped that he would find her in good health after all these years.

Sure enough, as Jesus finally caught sight of the house, there was the widow calmly sweeping her porch. She seemed much more relaxed than when he had first seen her nearly ten years earlier.

"Peace," said Jesus as he drew near.

The widow interrupted her sweeping and, resting on the handle of her broom, looked carefully at the man who had addressed her.

"And peace be with you," she finally said cautiously.

Jesus smiled at her and approached a little closer.

"It's you!" said the widow as her eyes glassed over in joyous recognition. "I thought I recognized your voice, but at first I just couldn't believe my eyes. How long has it been?"

"Nearly ten years," said Jesus. "I'm glad to see that you are healthy and much more relaxed than you were the last time I saw you."

"I am very healthy. And thanks to your kind encouragement, I am content," said the widow.

"So I take it that you did not give up on your appeals to the judge," said Jesus.

"Absolutely not. As you suggested, I just kept going back and going back. Believe it or not," said the widow, "he finally agreed to hear my case because he was afraid I would attack him. Me! A little old lady!"

"Whatever the reason, I'm glad that justice has been served," said Jesus. "In fact, as I left you that day I knew in my heart that your hunger for justice would be filled."

"And thanks to your encouragement all those years ago, it was. But how thoughtless of me!" exclaimed the widow. "You must be hungry and thirsty. Please come in. I don't have much more than I had the last time, but you are welcome to share what I have."

Jesus gladly accepted the invitation. It felt good to see a familiar face once more. He now knew that his journey was almost over, and that he was getting close to home.

Chapter 13

Jesus Returns to his Home in Nazareth

"Mother?" called Jesus as he stooped to enter the low doorway of the house in which he had once lived with his mother and Joseph before beginning his travels. "Mother?" called Jesus again when he heard no reply.

The house was not large, and it didn't take Jesus long to realize that Mary was not there. He then made his way to the workshop. That door, however, was secured with a peg. Jesus removed the peg and carefully pulled the door open. The workshop was dark. As his eyes adjusted to the dim light in the room, he began to notice that no projects seemed to be in progress. Dust covered the workbenches and all the tools were stored neatly on their racks. Joseph had obviously not worked on anything new for quite a while.

As Jesus was returning to the house, he saw his mother approaching carrying a jug of water from the well.

"Mother!" called Jesus as he ran to help her. "Here, let me carry that for you."

"Jesus, my son!" said Mary as she handed him the jug before giving him a tearful embrace.

"Mother, why are you carrying your own water from the well? Where is Joseph? Has he gone on another trip?"

"Joseph has died," said Mary in a quiet, somber tone. "I have been managing on my own for a while now, and I carry no more water than I am able. But, come. You must be hungry. Let me fix us something to eat and you can tell me all about your travels."

Back in the house, Jesus eagerly helped his mother with the preparations of the food and set two plates on the table.

"How did Joseph die?" asked Jesus.

"An illness. He was a strong man and worked hard until the end. At first, he refused to admit that there was anything wrong and continued his work each day although I could see that he was becoming weaker and less able to handle heavy jobs. He was almost sixty years old. The day finally came when he could not get out of bed. I kept him as comfortable as possible and encouraged him to eat and drink, but his spirit grew weaker each day. He asked about you always. We both were anxious to receive word from you."

"I'm sorry if I worried you. My Father in Heaven cared for me as he always does, as I am sure he watched out over the two of you in my absence."

"I reminded Joseph that you said you would be home soon as you had promised, but he was just too weak to go on. He insisted that I keep his tools safe for you."

For a long while Jesus and Mary sat in silence as they each recalled their individual memories of this great man who had so lovingly cared for both of them.

Jesus spent the next week or so resting up and helping his mother fix up small things around the house that needed repair or improvement. They spent hours bringing each other up to date, Mary telling her son all of the important things that happened in Nazareth and with their friends, and Jesus sharing the many things he had seen and learned on his travels.

"And are you now ready to begin your work as the Messiah to God's people?" asked Mary.

"Just about," said Jesus.

"Do you think that what you are about to do will cause those who believe in you to be scorned by others?" asked Mary.

"No doubt, Mother," said Jesus. "But I also believe that those people who are scorned on my account will be blessed by my Father and that their reward in Heaven will be great. In fact, Mother, one of the first things I intend to do is explain to God's people my own views about which people I believe should be considered to be blessed by my Father in Heaven."

"Son," said Mary, "I think that before you do anything, you ought to go and visit your cousin John."

"You mean you want me to travel to the house of your cousin Elizabeth where you went before I was born?"

"No," smiled Mary, "you won't have to travel that far. John is nearby."

"Where is he?" asked Jesus.

"He can be found at the Jordan River everyday."

"And what is he doing at the river?"

"He is delivering what he believes is a very important message from God to all who will listen. The poor thing is living on locusts and honey. I've tried to bring him better food to eat, but he simply gives it away to those who come out to listen to him."

"What message is he delivering?" asked Jesus.

"He is encouraging people to turn away from their sins because the Kingdom of God is at hand."

"And, indeed it is," said Jesus. "I believe my Father in Heaven is now calling me to begin my work. I will go to the Jordan River and visit my cousin very soon."

It was easy for Jesus to locate John along the Jordan. All he had to do was follow a steady stream of people that went daily to see him and listen to his message. When Jesus came within sight of his cousin, he stopped to watch and listen.

He saw that as each person approached John to proclaim that he was ready to turn away from sin and live a life of preparation for the Kingdom of Heaven, he would be dipped into the water by John. Just as those who entered a Roman bath house first passed through a shallow cleansing pool called a *Baptisterium*, John was using this ceremonial dipping as a sign that the person was cleansed of his sins. Each person, wet and smiling, emerged happy to begin his new life.

Jesus moved closer to the shore and got in line.

When Jesus finally approached his cousin, John stopped and looked at him in amazement. They had not seen each other for many years, but John knew exactly who the young man was that was standing before him.

"I ought to be cleansed by you," began John in a low voice, "and yet you have come to me?"

"Let's do it this way for now," said Jesus. "This way we'll be doing all that God requires."

As Jesus came up out of the water, all those gathered on the shore were amazed to see the heavens appear to open above them. As the attention of John and the others was drawn to Jesus, a dove flew down out of the sky and landed on his right shoulder.

Suddenly, a thunderous voice from above filled the valley.

"This is my own Beloved Son," proclaimed the mighty voice from the sky, "with whom I am very pleased. Listen to him!"

Chapter 14

The Beginning

And thus began the public life of Jesus as Immanuel, the Messiah both to the Israelites and the Gentiles.

Jesus would have only three years in which to accomplish his mission.

His divinity as the Son of God on earth seems definitely to be confirmed by the fact that within those three short years Jesus established a ministry that even to this day continues to proclaim and share the Good News of his Father in Heaven to all that will hear it and accept Him as their Savior.

Incipio Est!

Map for Raising Jesus, the Early Years

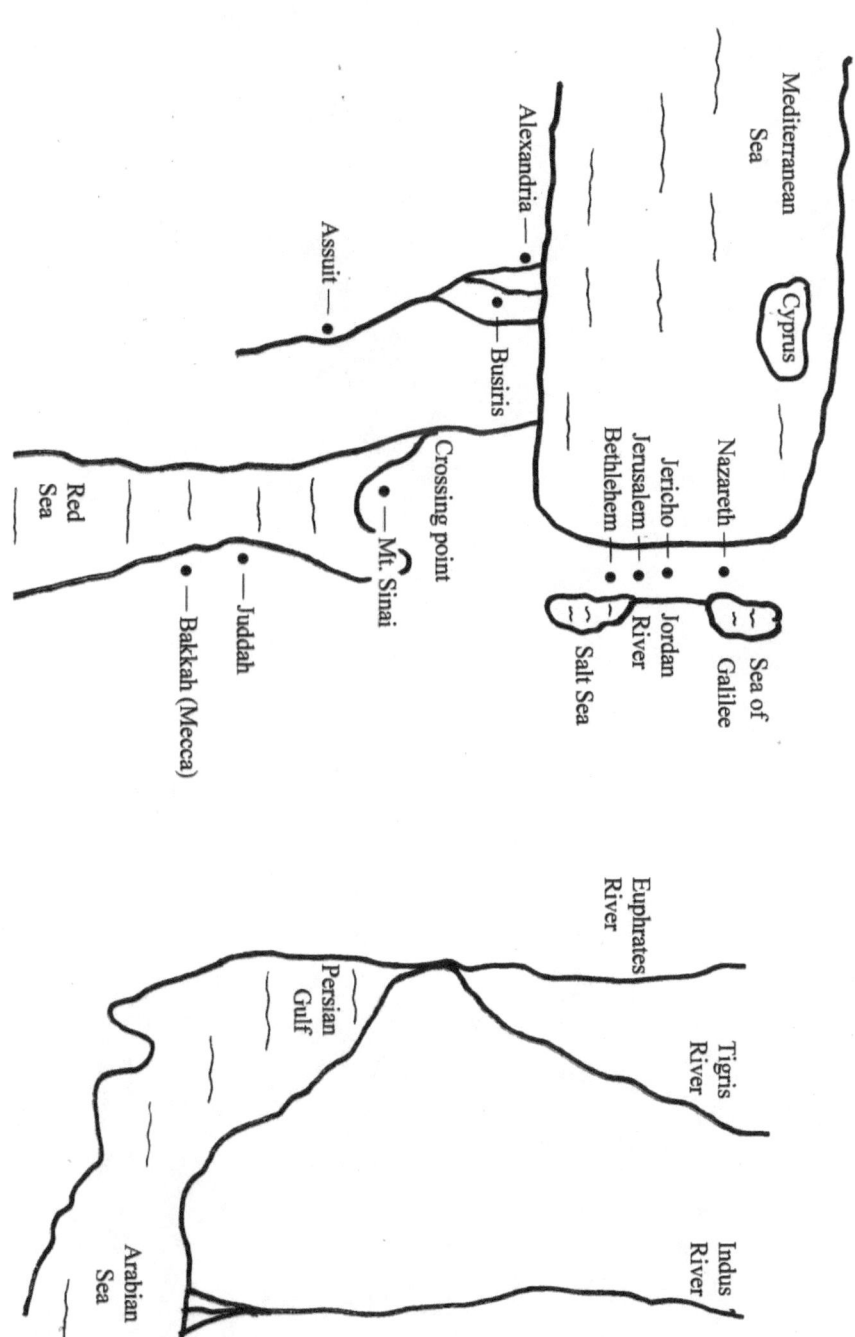

Constance